‖‖‖‖‖‖‖‖‖‖‖‖‖‖‖‖‖‖‖‖‖‖‖‖‖‖‖

W9-BXY-615

2010

The Door Burst Inward . . .

The entire room shook as splinters sprayed in all directions
and the iron latch clattered across the floor. Yelling at the
tops of his lungs, a short, stocky gent bounded into the
room holding a Colt pistol in each hand. He swung toward
Longarm's bed. Arizona lifted her head and screamed.

Longarm tripped the shotgun's left trigger. The thundering roar filled the entire room and rocked the walls. The
eight-gauge double-aught buckshot clubbed the would-be
assassin in the middle of his shirt, lifting him straight out of
his boots. His arms flew toward the ceiling, and both pistols
popped at the same time, their bullets plunking the ceiling
above the bed. Longarm caught a glimpse of another man
behind the first—just before the first smashed back into the
second, who yelped and hit the hall floor on his back.

"Ay, mi Dios!" Arizona cried, scrambling out from under Longarm and clinging with one hand to the headboard
as if to a sinking ship.

The second man wailed and blew blood from his lips as
he lifted one of his two pistols . . .

**DON'T MISS THESE
ALL-ACTION WESTERN SERIES
FROM THE BERKLEY PUBLISHING GROUP**

THE GUNSMITH by J. R. Roberts
Clint Adams was a legend among lawmen, outlaws, and ladies. They called him . . . the Gunsmith.

LONGARM by Tabor Evans
The popular long-running series about Deputy U.S. Marshal Custis Long—his life, his loves, his fight for justice.

SLOCUM by Jake Logan
Today's longest-running action Western. John Slocum rides a deadly trail of hot blood and cold steel.

BUSHWHACKERS by B. J. Lanagan
An action-packed series by the creators of Longarm! The rousing adventures of the most brutal gang of cutthroats ever assembled—Quantrill's Raiders.

DIAMONDBACK by Guy Brewer
Dex Yancey is Diamondback, a Southern gentleman turned con man when his brother cheats him out of the family fortune. Ladies love him. Gamblers hate him. But nobody pulls one over on Dex . . .

WILDGUN by Jack Hanson
The blazing adventures of mountain man Will Barlow— from the creators of Longarm!

TEXAS TRACKER by Tom Calhoun
J.T. Law: the most relentless—and dangerous—manhunter in all Texas. Where sheriffs and posses fail, he's the best man to bring in the most vicious outlaws—for a price.

→→ TABOR EVANS ←←

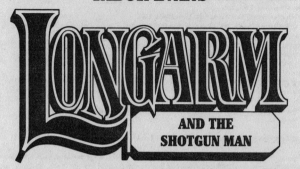

LONGARM

AND THE SHOTGUN MAN

J

JOVE BOOKS, NEW YORK

Sandy Public Library

THE BERKLEY PUBLISHING GROUP
Published by the Penguin Group
Penguin Group (USA) Inc.
375 Hudson Street, New York, New York 10014, USA
Penguin Group (Canada), 90 Eglinton Avenue East, Suite 700, Toronto, Ontario M4P 2Y3, Canada
(a division of Pearson Penguin Canada Inc.)
Penguin Books Ltd., 80 Strand, London WC2R 0RL, England
Penguin Group Ireland, 25 St. Stephen's Green, Dublin 2, Ireland (a division of Penguin Books Ltd.)
Penguin Group (Australia), 250 Camberwell Road, Camberwell, Victoria 3124, Australia
(a division of Pearson Australia Group Pty. Ltd.)
Penguin Books India Pvt. Ltd., 11 Community Centre, Panchsheel Park, New Delhi—110 017, India
Penguin Group (NZ), 67 Apollo Drive, Rosedale, North Shore 0632, New Zealand
(a division of Pearson New Zealand Ltd.)
Penguin Books (South Africa) (Pty.) Ltd., 24 Sturdee Avenue, Rosebank, Johannesburg 2196,
South Africa

Penguin Books Ltd., Registered Offices: 80 Strand, London WC2R 0RL, England

This is a work of fiction. Names, characters, places, and incidents either are the product of the author's imagination or are used fictitiously, and any resemblance to actual persons, living or dead, business establishments, events, or locales is entirely coincidental.

LONGARM AND THE SHOTGUN MAN

A Jove Book / published by arrangement with the author

PRINTING HISTORY
Jove edition / September 2009

Copyright © 2009 by Penguin Group (USA) Inc.
Cover illustration by Miro Sinovcic.

All rights reserved.
No part of this book may be reproduced, scanned, or distributed in any printed or electronic form without permission. Please do not participate in or encourage piracy of copyrighted materials in violation of the author's rights. Purchase only authorized editions.
For information, address: The Berkley Publishing Group,
a division of Penguin Group (USA) Inc.,
375 Hudson Street, New York, New York 10014.

ISBN: 978-0-515-14693-6

JOVE®
Jove Books are published by The Berkley Publishing Group,
a division of Penguin Group (USA) Inc.,
375 Hudson Street, New York, New York 10014.
JOVE® is a registered trademark of Penguin Group (USA) Inc.
The "J" design is a trademark of Penguin Group (USA) Inc.

PRINTED IN THE UNITED STATES OF AMERICA

10 9 8 7 6 5 4 3 2 1

If you purchased this book without a cover, you should be aware that this book is stolen property. It was reported as "unsold and destroyed" to the publisher, and neither the author nor the publisher has received any payment for this "stripped book."

Chapter 1

There was a low, raspy whine, like a witch's hum.

It grew quickly louder until it snapped a small tree branch just right of the trail. The bullet pierced the crown of the lawman's hat with the menacingly soft gasp of a jealous lover, and then pinged off a rock on the trail's other side.

The whip-crack of the rifle followed half an eyeblink later.

A quarter second after that, Deputy U.S. Marshal Custis Long, known as Longarm to friend and foe, threw himself off the back of the army bay he'd acquisitioned from Camp Collins sixty miles north of Denver. With a curse, he hit the ground on his left shoulder and hip, and rolled.

He'd only meant to roll a few yards, down below a hummock that would offer cover from the bushwhacker on the ridge above him. But the slope was steeper than he'd figured, and he found himself rolling out of control, arms and legs flying, his brown corduroy coat and his string tie flapping wildly. He heard himself grunting and groaning as the steep, uneven ground battered him, and he heard the thumps of his low-heeled cavalry boots hammering the ground in turn.

From above, he could hear the bay whinnying as it took flight across the shoulder of the ridge below the aspens, the sound of its thudding hooves quickly dwindling.

During one of his brain-addling rotations, Longarm spied a relatively flat gravelly shoulder pushing up fast from below. He'd barely had time to feel relieved that the end of his frenzied descent was in sight when the shelf was suddenly beneath him.

His descent slowed.

Gravity tugged at him for a few seconds more, and then he rolled one more time and found himself facedown in sand and gravel. Too late, he realized that his knees were hanging over a steep ledge—one he hadn't seen but now remembered riding around on his way up the ridge—and before he could try to push himself away from the precipice, he was dropping over it, following his plunging boots.

His stomach slammed up into his throat, and he gasped, flailing up and away from his chest with his hands. He found a hold before he realized it—the very edge of the sheer, sandstone scarp—and dug his fingers in, his guts floating around inside him as his fingertips slipped and slid on the fine grains of sand between them and solid sandstone.

His fingers slid to the edge of the rock. They wouldn't hold him.

Frantically, he looked around for another stay. Then, praying he could hold himself for a few seconds with his left hand in that precarious position, he dropped the right about a foot and grabbed a knob about the size and shape of a wheel hub. At the same time, he ground his boots against the wall, probing cracks, fissures, and protruding rock thumbs with his toes.

As he wedged his left boot against a narrow shelf, he lowered his left hand to a crack, grinding his aching fingers into the tiny defile for purchase. Knowing the holds weren't solid enough to pull him back up, he headed down the bricklike wall of sandstone toward the sandy, scrub-covered slope sixty feet below.

As he did, he heard voices on the ridge above—the excited exclamations of the men who'd bushwhacked him as they made their way down the ridge, likely searching for their quarry.

If they found Longarm on the wall, he'd be pot-shot wolf bait. As he dropped another few feet, gritting his teeth as he fought for holds, he glanced down at his left hip.

The cross-draw holster was empty. He must have lost his double-action Frontier model Colt .44 during the roll down the mountain.

Son of a bitch.

He was halfway down the wall when he spied a small, jagged hole to his right. Holding himself with his left hand and both boots, one above the other and about three feet apart, he shoved his right hand into the hole.

It donned on him a quarter second before he did it that he should have investigated the hole first. Not even a copper-riveted tinhorn would go blindly poking his hand in a rocky crevice. The admonishing hiss that rose from the niche validated the notion. But he'd already put his weight on his right hand, removing the left from the ledge just above his shoulder.

The maneuver brought him face-to-face with the diamondback that was coiled about six inches behind his right hand, the pointed tip of its rattle poking above its nine or ten angrily quivering buttons.

The snake's flat head rose as it moved toward Longarm,

its forked tongue testing the air, its menacing eyes like miniature pistol bores aimed at his nose.

Longarm's heart leaped as the head shot toward him—a silver green blur.

"Christ!"

He removed his right hand from the hole.

But not before the snake had sunk its long, razor-edged fangs into his cheek, just below his eye.

He jerked his head back. The snake came with him, rattling and writhing, the fangs clinging to his cheek—an ice-hot pain that set his entire head on fire.

His boots slipped off the wall and he found himself shooting straight down the ridge's craggy face, the snake swirling through the air in front of him until it managed to free its fangs from the lawman's leathery hide.

Then, because everything became a blur, he wasn't sure what happened to the snake.

His last sensation was the ground coming up to slam against his boots so hard that he heard his jaws clack together and felt his ribs splinter as his hips were driven up into his belly.

Then his head sank back in a spindly sage bush—he smelled the dusty tang in his nostrils—and merciful darkness washed over him like tar.

Broom Tanner knelt beside a boulder sheathed in brush, and poked his scrubby hat back off his sweaty forehead as he stared down the slope below him.

He glanced to his right and, grinning delightedly, beckoned to his partner, "Black Jack" Baumgartner, who was scouting the slope a hundred yards east at a crouch, his funnel-brimmed hat pulled low, his Spencer rifle held high across his chest in both hands.

When Black Jack, so known for his long, stringy black hair and matching, oily black eyes, stood beside Tanner, Tanner canted his head down the slope and stretched his lips back from his long, tobacco-stained teeth that resembled frost-heaved fence posts spouting from a muddy bog.

"There he is," Tanner said, wheezing a laugh. "Right down there!"

"Holy shit up a nun's caboose!" exclaimed Black Jack under his breath. He dropped to a knee, ran the back of his wrist across his snotty nose, and stared at the tall man stretched out in the sage below the sandstone shelf. "Looks like a whiskey drummer. Maybe a gambler. Look at that jacket and that vest. Is that a gold watch chain?"

"Looks gold to me," said Tanner, the dry wind blowing his silver hair and matching shaggy beard. Wearing the rose-colored glasses he'd pulled off the last pilgrim he and Black Jack had robbed and killed in this remote stretch of the northern Rockies, he nodded. "Wonder what else he's got on him."

"Prob'ly plenty," Black Jack said. "And there's his horse up yonder—a fine-lookin' critter. I bet he's got a dollar or two in his saddlebags. Believe I seen a war bag hangin' from his saddle, too!"

Tanner looked around, making sure the lone rider was indeed alone and not part of a larger, scattered party. Spying nothing but low, jagged ridges, scattered pinyons, and sage, he glanced at Black Jack, his leathery cheeks flushed with excitement. "Didn't I tell you this would be a whole lot easier than prospectin'?"

"You did at that, cousin." Black Jack chuckled and straightened, raising his rifle. "You did at that."

"What're you doin?"

"Gonna make sure the bastard's dead."

"Shit, save your bullets." Tanner started tramping down the slope, holding his own Winchester low at his side in one hand. "Bastard rolled off that scarp there. Gotta be a hundred-foot drop. If he ain't dead, St. Pete can hear him comin'."

Tanner moved down the slope, taking mincing steps on the steepest part of the slope so he didn't fall on his ass. His boot soles were worn nearly all the way through to his socks. He was eyeing the boots of his victim, trying to gauge their size.

That coat and them boots would look mighty good on Tanner. If he was sporting duds like those, Miss Madeline over to Lyons might be more willing to allow him into her whorehouse. Of course, he'd have to remember not to spit chaw on her Persian rugs, but first things first . . .

He approached his victim slowly, taking his Winchester in both hands. Black Jack moved up beside him, aiming his Spencer straight out from his hip.

The man before them lay unmoving on his back—a tall, broad-shouldered, trim-waisted hombre with thick brown hair, brown longhorn mustache, and finely chiseled cheeks burned the shade of old saddle leather. There were two small holes in the nub of his left cheek, each showing a bright little blood bead.

He wore a fawn wool vest over a white shirt, and his skintight whipcord trousers were stuffed into the tops of his mule-eared, low-heeled cavalry boots.

"I'll be damned," Black Jack said. "That's one well-set-up hombre. A moneyed man, if'n I ever seen one. Not only a gambler—but a *good* gambler. Ha!"

"Check his pockets, Jack. I'll keep an eye on him, make sure he don't come alive of a sudden." Tanner shifted his weight eagerly from one foot to the other, and squeezed his rifle in his hands. "I got dibs on his coat and boots."

"I got his shirt," Black Jack said. "Shit, looks damn near new!"

As Black Jack dropped to a knee beside the unmoving hombre, he set his rifle on the ground and began going through the man's trouser pockets. As he did, the man's right arm fell back onto the ground. Tanner saw something gold wink at him from between the fingers of the man's closed hand. A gold watch lay nearby, the chain of which was connected to whatever the man was holding in his fist.

"Hey, Jack," Tanner said, his mouth watering at the very notion of gold. His rose-colored spectacles slid down his nose. "What's that he's got in his hand? Check it out!"

Black Jack had just pulled a small wad of bills from the man's trouser pocket. Now he glanced up at Tanner. "Huh?"

"Check his hand, Jack! Check his hand!"

"All right, all right," grunted Jack. "I'll check his hand."

Dropping the wadded greenbacks, Jack leaned across the man's torso, reaching with both his own hands for the man's right one.

"You don't have to do that, Jack."

The unfamiliar voice—low and slightly raspy—froze both men. Jack jerked his head up at Tanner, his shaggy black brows furrowed with befuddlement. Tanner returned the look.

"Huh?" Tanner said.

He took one nervous step back, raising his Winchester's barrel. At the same time, Tanner looked down at their victim. The man's right hand was open. The hand was holding a cocked, gold-chased, over-and-under derringer. From the butt of the pearl-gripped popper, the gold-washed chain and dented gold watch dangled.

The man's brown eyes were open. They were hard, and they were staring at Jack.

"Back away, Jack," the man said, so tightly that his thick brown mustache barely moved above his upper lip. "Do it now and do it slow, or I'll give you a third eye—a blind one." His gaze slid to Tanner though he kept the derringer trained on Jack. "You, amigo—throw down that Winchester."

Tanner stood frozen. Below him, facing their "victim," Jack tensed. Slowly, Jack turned his head to look up at Tanner. Above his beard, his face was mottled pink, and his black eyes were scared.

"He's only got that little peashooter," Tanner said, his heart hammering his ribs. "Shit, how much damage can he do with that?"

"Enough, you tinhorn!" the prostrate hombre rasped.

Tanner frenziedly shuttled his gaze between the gun and the man's face. The peashooter was aimed at Black Jack, not Tanner.

Whooping like a lobo, Tanner jerked his Winchester toward the man's head. At the same time, the peashooter popped. Tanner felt a sharp hitch in his chest.

The Winchester thundered, but the .44-caliber slug that had just smashed through Tanner's breastbone had nudged his shot into the ground over the prostrate hombre's right shoulder.

Tanner dropped the gun and stumbled straight back, his glasses hanging by one ear. His shattered heart had stopped beating before he hit the ground. At the same time, Longarm turned his derringer back left, toward the man called Black Jack, who was diving for his rifle. Longarm half closed one eye as he calmly aimed and squeezed the trigger.

Pop!

Black Jack crumpled over his rifle, quivering, the .44-caliber hole over his right ear dribbling blood down his neck.

Longarm pushed up on his elbows and kicked Black Jack off his own left ankle.

Sitting up, Longarm brushed blood from his snakebit cheek with the hand that held the smoking popper, and glanced at the dead men. He sighed.

"Fuckin' morons."

Chapter 2

Longarm wrestled up onto his knees, wincing against the pain he felt in every joint in his battered body.

He'd been sure he'd come out of the fall from the rock wall with two broken hips if not two shattered legs, but while he felt as though his lower extremities had been used by a passel of Apache braves for bow-and-arrow practice, he didn't feel any broken bones grinding around.

He set his boots beneath him, balancing carefully on both hands, and put pressure first on his ankles, then his legs. When he'd straightened his knees and stood looking around, taking deep, easy breaths, relief washed over him.

Nothing felt broken. He might have a cracked rib or two, and his left shoulder was rickety, but he was lucky. If he'd suffered a broken hip or a broken leg out here, with his horse having run off, he'd have been crow bait for sure.

He probed his cheek with his fingers. The bite from the coiled demon in the rocks above had numbed his cheek, and there was some swelling around the two puncture wounds. But again, he was lucky. If the snake had injected him with its toxic venom, his head would be swollen up like salt lick by now. The viper must have fed recently, expending its venon on a rabbit or such, and hadn't had time to refill its well, so to speak.

Longarm chuffed and shook his head. He didn't deserve such luck.

He glanced again at the dead men bleeding out in the sage around him. Then he looked up the ridge, toward the mixed pines and aspens climbing steeply toward the rocky saddle a good mile above. He'd been heading for the saddle, on his way to the little Wyoming mountain town of Rabbit Ridge, when the two highwaymen had drygulched him. It looked like his horse had run a good ways off, might even be on the other side of the ridge by now.

Still, he thought, walking around on his creaky but unbroken legs, gently testing his ankles, he was damn lucky.

He'd spied a creek running through the gorge just below him. He'd wander on down to the water, bathe his cheek to hold the swelling at bay, and have a long drink. Then, after a rest to clear the cobwebs from his head and the aches from his body, he'd go on up and try to retrieve his horse before nightfall.

He'd scheduled a meeting in Rabbit Ridge at tomorrow noon. With this little setback, he'd be a few hours late. If he didn't find the bay, he'd be later than that. Unless he appropriated the mounts of the dead trail robbers . . .

He shaded his eyes as he scrutinized the ridge. They must have a couple of mounts tethered up in the forest somewhere, probably out of sight behind that rocky knob a couple of hundred feet up and jutting above the aspens that were just now beginning to boast some fall-yellow amongst their lime green leaves.

Longarm reloaded his derringer, and slid it back into his vest pocket. He shoved his old Ingersoll watch into the other one, the chain connecting the two dangling across his belly. He picked up the Winchester of the owlhoot called Tanner, wiped the fresh blood from its stock, then glanced around for the snake. Doing so, he spied his double-action Colt .44 lying between sage shrubs, and stooped to pick it up, cleaning the trusty weapon against his corduroy coat. The gun must have rolled with him down over the ridge.

Straightening and dropping the Colt in the cross-draw holster on his left hip, and snapping the keeper thong over the hammer, he glanced up the steep, crenelated rock wall once more. Nausea billowed around in his guts as he judged the distance he'd fallen—in tandem with a snake, no less . . .

He chuckled wryly at either his good luck or bad— suddenly, he wasn't sure which—then, holding the dead man's rifle over his shoulder, began limping down the long slope toward the aspen-choked gorge directly below. He took his time, wincing at the creaking in his bones, feeling his right knee start to bark and his head start to swim.

He was probably more addled than he'd at first been aware. Ah, well—nothing a couple shots of Maryland rye wouldn't cure.

But he'd have to run his horse down first, because his burlap-swathed bottle was nestled in his saddlebags, which, in turn, were draped over the bay's hindquarters.

Shit.

When Longarm had negotiated the brush, rocks, and trees at the gorge's bottom, he dropped down beside the creek twisting through its gravel bed. The shallow water clinked like coins on a gambling table, flashing in the late afternoon sunlight. The far wall of the gorge was nearly as steep as the ridge he'd fallen from, but pocked here and there with shrubs and sliderock.

He lay on his belly and lowered his face to the cool, sliding water. The snakebite throbbed at first, but then the water worked its magic and the pain dulled. He opened his mouth, taking several long pulls, and the drink as well as the bath made him feel better.

On his knees, hands on his thighs, he took several deep, refreshing breaths, water dribbling down his cheeks and soaked mustache. Then he leaned forward for another drink.

Behind him, a horse snorted. There was the dull thud of hooves.

Longarm lifted his head suddenly. He pushed up to his haunches, twisting around and peering back through the breeze-jostled branches.

A rider was moving slowly down the slope behind him, leading an extra horse.

The lawman grabbed his Colt from its holster, and scuttled up to a broad cottonwood between himself and the rider. He pressed his back against the trunk, and held his cocked .44 barrel up by his shoulder, tense and waiting.

Was there a third cutthroat?

Turning his head to one side, he listened as the hoof clomps and squawking tack grew louder. Brush crunched beneath the horses' hooves, and bridle chains rattled faintly.

To Longarm's left, a large shadow moved over the wheatgrass and rocks, and then the head of a buckskin horse appeared, pushing between the trees. Longarm stepped out from behind the cottonwood and extended the Colt straight out from his right shoulder, thumbing the hammer back with a loud, ratcheting click.

The rider moved into the clearing and came into view atop his horse.

Her horse.

The girl's eyes widened when they found Longarm aiming the cocked Colt at her head, and she drew back abruptly on the reins of her tall, clean-lined buckskin. The horse behind her was Longarm's own army bay. She held its bridle reins in her left hand, her own reins in her right.

"Who the hell're you?" Longarm said, feeling a thickness in his throat as his eyes took the girl's quick measure and found her not wanting in the least when it came to beauty.

She was a brown-eyed blonde with a red calico blouse unbuttoned halfway down her chest and a soft doeskin riding skirt, the slit of which revealed a good portion of well-turned, smooth, perfectly tanned thigh. Her face was heart-shaped and full-lipped, with a small, perfect nose. Her eyes were wide and clear, and her blond hair blew out from the brown leather hat tipped back off her forehead.

Eighteen or nineteen, Longarm judged. Not a year over twenty. But she more than adequately filled out the calico blouse that one would more likely expect on an Apache squaw. She wore moccasin boots, too, and a rawhide pouch—like a medicine bag—hung down over the full, enticing swell of her breasts.

"Well, don't shoot me for chrissakes!" she admonished, frowning suddenly, a flush rising in those smooth, tapering cheeks. "I don't mean no harm. I just found this horse up yonder, and figured he belonged to you."

"How'd you figure?"

"I heard the shooting from higher up. When I came down to the edge of the trees, I seen you limping down the hill." Her eyes flashed impatient fire. "Well, is he or ain't he?"

Longarm depressed the Colt's hammer, and lowered the gun to his side. "He is." His eyes raked the girl's delectable frame once more. She was like the sunshine of a thousand glorious mountain mornings sitting atop that old Texas saddle. He felt his face relax, and a smile tugged at his mouth. "I'm much obliged to you, Miss . . ."

"Spurlock." She tossed his reins to him, and he caught them with his free hand against his chest. "Rye Spurlock." Her own coolly appraising gaze flickered up and down Longarm's tall, lean, broad-shouldered frame with subtle female interest. "I seen the dead men as I rode down. You kill 'em?"

"They didn't give me a whole lotta choice."

"Figures. This is bad country. When I heard the shootin', I figured it wasn't just range riders pot-shooting coyotes. Had a bad feelin', I did." Rye Spurlock leaned forward on her saddle horn, sort of hiked her shoulders coquettishly, and canted her head to one side as she raked her smoky brown eyes across him once more. "For such a fine-dressed gent, you ain't very polite."

"How's that?"

"You ain't told me your name, and you ain't asked me to light and help myself to some water. Both my canteens is empty. And I *did* just retrieve your horse. He'd have been a long ways gone if I hadn't spied him and run him down."

Longarm chuckled and noted a serious abatement in the pain of his injuries. Even in the two puncture wounds in his face. If one could bottle the essence of the fine, blond-haired, brown-eyed beauty before him, including her buoyant, invigorating spirit, there'd be no need for the medical profession. "Name's Gus," Longarm said, using one of the aliases he often employed when he was out on undercover assignment, as he was now. "Gus Short. Call me Gus."

The girl stretched those exquisite lips in a wistful grin and swung lightly out of her saddle. "Call me Rye." She gave her reins a playful little spin, and let them fall to the ground behind her as she strolled over to the creek, swinging her hips and letting her rich hair bounce on her shoulders, and dropped to her knees. "What are you doing out here, Gus—if you don't mind my askin'? That cheek of yourn looks a mite on the painful side."

As she doffed her hat and leaned forward to splash water on her face, Longarm sauntered back over to where he'd been partaking of the cool creek water himself, and dropped to his knees. "I'm headin' up to Rabbit Ridge. Gonna take a job there, if it's still open." He soaked a handkerchief and dabbed at his cheek, his eyes riveted on the intoxicating girl splashing away in the creek about ten feet to his left. "You?"

"Headed in the same direction," she said between splashes. Then she dropped down to her belly and lowered her face to the cool water. Her blond hair swirled around her head in the sliding current. She drank for a time, slurping and groaning and wriggling around in the dust and grass, until Longarm felt his loins throb with goatish, automatic desire.

Then she jerked her head up suddenly, eyes round and wary.

Water dribbled down her face and onto her calico blouse as she rose to her knees and looked beyond Longarm, toward the main trail. "I'm on the run, as a matter of fact. A man's after me. A greasy snake who dresses all in black, from his hat to his black leather pants. Name's Cormorant." Her eyes jerked to Longarm's. "Ever hear of him, Gus?"

Longarm shook his head as he glanced over his shoulder in the direction the girl was looking. "Can't say as I have."

"He's tall and thin, talks like this," she said while stretching her lips wide and speaking tightly, as though her jaws were broken.

Breaking the impersonation off abruptly, she leaned down to slurp at the water hungrily once more, grinding her hips in the dirt. Raising her dripping face to stare off across the creek, she swept her hair away from her face with one hand. "He's a pistolero. Regulator. A good one, too." She choked a little on the water. "Too damn good."

"Why's this Cormorant fella got it in for you? You don't look like the type to piss-burn anyone, Miss Rye. Let alone a killer for hire."

A bird piped somewhere behind Longarm. The girl's head jerked up, and she gasped. "What was that? Did you hear it?"

Again, Longarm looked behind him. "Just a bird, Miss Rye."

"It *sounded* like a bird." She was whispering now, her back taut, her arms crossed over her breasts as she stared through the breeze-brushed trees. "He can do that—make sounds like birds. He's got Injun blood. Half Apache!"

Longarm looked at the girl. She was genuinely frightened. The horses behind her, however, grazed contentedly. Just the same, Longarm palmed his Colt and rose to his feet.

"Why don't I check it out?"

As he moved slowly off through the brush, the falling sun showing golden through the darkening branches, the girl hissed at his back, "Be careful, Mr. Short."

"Gus," Longarm corrected gently.

"I mean Gus," she whispered. "He's a demon. He truly is!"

"I'll take that into consideration," Longarm said, striding

slowly off through the cottonwoods, angling away from the creek.

Longarm's ears had been trained by years of manhunting to pick up the faintest sounds around him, and to distinguish one from another. All he heard out here, however, was the gurgling and metallic clinking of the creek over the rocks, the swish of the breeze-ruffled leaves and grass, and the pipings of birds.

He moved toward a juniper. He'd tramp just that far, and if he didn't see a black-clad gunman named Cormorant by then, he'd turn around and head back to the creek and the girl.

He stepped around the juniper.

There was a sudden scurrying sound in the brush to his left. A loud snort. A loud thump.

Spying movement in the corner of his left eye, Longarm brought his Colt up quickly and wheeled.

Chapter 3

Longarm's heart leaped with a start. He squinted one eye and aimed.

He held fire when he saw that what his .44's sights were trained on was the slender, white-ringed, black-tailed ass of a mule deer. The doe bounded off through the brush away from him, and before he even had time to lower the Colt, the doe dropped down a slight depression sheathed in willows and disappeared.

Its hooves thudded, crunching brush and scuffing rocks.

Longarm depressed the Colt's hammer with a relieved sigh, and took one more quick look around. Dropping the Colt back into its holster and snapping the keeper thong over the hammer, he strode back to where the girl knelt beside the creek, holding a wide-bladed bowie knife in both hands up in front of her chest. Her lustrous brown eyes flashed warily above the upturned end of the knife, which looked inordinately large in the girl's slender, gloved hands.

"Did you see him?" she said, her voice shrill with worry.

Longarm shook his head. "Just a deer." He stopped in

front of her, and gave a sardonic chuff. "Where in the hell did you get that?"

She looked up at him from beneath her sandy brows. "I'm afraid of guns. Can't stand the bang of 'em. So I carry this thing." She dipped her chin seriously. "I'm good with it, too."

"Something tells me you would be."

She opened the slit in her calfskin skirt, revealing a smoked deerskin sheath strapped to her comely right calf. She slid the knife into the sheath, glancing up at Longarm. "You sure Cormorant ain't out there stealin' around?"

"Pretty damn sure. Besides, unless he's bathed recently, our mounts would have winded him." Longarm turned and began walking toward the horses, both still grazing peacefully. "I reckon I'll camp here for the night, get an early start in the mornin'. You're welcome to stay here, too, if you're of a mind." He didn't really want the pretty girl around, tormenting him with her sexy beauty and charm—she was too young and honey-sweet to make a play for—but it was only right to make the offer.

He grabbed his saddlebags off the bay's back, draped the pouches over his shoulder, and strode back over to the girl, who was still kneeling beside the creek. She was looking around carefully.

"I reckon I'll stay with you, Gus." Rye Spurlock gave him the up-and-down once more. "If you won't think me fresh."

"I won't think you fresh, if you don't think it of me." Longarm pulled his bottle of Maryland rye from his saddlebags, and held up the bottle. "Shall we drink to it?"

"Oh, Jesus and St. Christopher!" the girl trilled, pressing her hands flat against her breasts. "Could I use a belt!"

Longarm sat on a rock and fished a couple of tin cups

that had been scorched by the flames of many campfires out of his saddlebags. The girl sat on a rock to his left, and watched thirstily as he splashed his beloved Maryland rye into one cup, and handed it to her.

"Rye for Miss Rye."

She chuckled huskily. *"Muchas gracias, amigo!"*

As Longarm splashed the whiskey into his own cup, the girl lifted her drink to her lips slowly with both hands, sniffing deeply. She threw back a sizable shot quickly, and lifted her head. Her throat worked in her long, fine neck as she swallowed, closing her eyes.

"Oh . . ." She smacked her lips, a flush rising in her lightly suntanned cheeks. "That's good."

Longarm propped the bottle between his boots, and threw back a shot. He drew a deep breath, inhaling the rye's rich, intoxicating aroma while the liquid itself burned down his throat and into his belly, instantly easing the fire in his cheeks and the aches in his joints.

"No better hooch has yet been brewed." Setting his elbows on his knees, Longarm glanced at the girl, who sat back on her own rock, extending her legs and crossing her ankles. "Forgive me for prying, Miss Rye, but how is it you came to be tangled up with this lunatic Cormorant anyway?"

Rye Spurlock was still looking around cautiously, though not with the fearful vigor of a few minutes ago. "My father's a rancher from down around Sapinero, in southern Colorado. Cormorant works for him. Or, I should say, kills the sheepmen who've been crowding the edges of my father's range . . . and anyone else who deigns to tap a picket pin anywhere near the Double Chain-Link. We're from Texas, you see. Times were hard in the years after the War, when the carpetbaggers moved in and set up their own laws. Pa got tough and started keeping company with men like Weed Cormorant."

Longarm arched a brow. "Weed?"

Rye nodded as she turned to look back over her shoulder. "To make a long story short, Cormorant tried sparkin' me. Oh, I was fool enough to give him a poke once or twice. Shit, I was drunk and the stars were bright—that old saw. I figured once he'd gotten what he was after, he'd leave me alone."

She shook her head in disgust.

"No such luck. He started followin' me around Pa's range like a hind-tit calf. Even started shirkin' his own killin' duties to give me chase. Even serenaded me with a guitar one night, outside my bedroom in the main lodge!" Rye sighed and turned toward Longarm. "Well, Pa ordered me to marry the man. Said he'd made a deal with Cormorant, and I had no choice but to be joined to him in holy matrimony. Ha! Pa's as crazy as that half-Apache killer."

Rye threw back another sip of the rye and squeezed her eyes closed again as she swallowed. "This little gal was throwin' in on that deal. Life's too short to spend it with someone you don't love. Not only don't love, but despise!" She gave a little shiver and crossed her arms beneath her breasts. "The second time I let him touch me, I thought I'd be sick before it was over!"

"Sounds an awful lot to expect," Longarm opined. "Makin' your pretty young daughter hitch her star to a crazy regulator as part of some business deal."

"Glad you see it my way. You see"—Rye twirled her index finger in the air by her ear—"Pa's gone completely loco. Runs in his family. Just doesn't think straight, and I reckon there's nothin' to be done about it. That's why I'm here now, with no intention of ever returning to Sapinero. I'd kill myself first! My inheritance be damned!"

"So where you headed?" Longarm asked her after he'd polished off his own cup of whiskey and was reaching for the bottle at his feet.

"I'm goin' on up to Rabbit Ridge, and I'm gonna hop the stage for Crow Canyon on the other side of the Western Slope. Got me a boy there, don't you know. Used to break mustangs for my pa . . . till Pa caught us together. Didn't want me and Bob hitchin' up, because he said Bob didn't have no future except for a stove-in chest and scrambled brains. As if Cormorant is any better!"

"I'd imagine ole Weed might be better set up in the money department," Longarm quipped. "Depending on how many sheepmen he beefed in any given year, of course."

"He's better set up in the ugly department, too. He's even got a wooden hand." Rye gave a very good imitation of retching. "But Bob—he's all golden curls and blue eyes. Not nearly as tall and broad as you are, Gus, but he's cuter'n a speckled pup!"

"Congratulations, Miss Rye," Longarm said, pouring more rye into the girl's glass and glancing at her skeptically. She seemed no drunker than he was. Obviously, the girl had imbibed a few times before. "I wish you and ole Bob all the happiness in the world. Just so happens," he said, corking the bottle and lowering it back down to his boots, "I'm headed to the stage station in Rabbit Ridge my ownself. That's where I'm talkin' to a man about a job, matter of fact."

"With the stage?"

"They need a new a shotgun rider." Well, they didn't

really need a new one. The Clark & Kinney Great Divide Line already had one, though they'd been through four in the past six months—all four shotgun guards having been killed by owlhoots robbing the stage.

What the line did need, and had asked for, was federal help in running the owlhoots to ground. That's why Longarm's boss, Chief Marshal Billy Vail of the First District Court of Colorado in Denver, had sent Longarm up to Rabbit Ridge to ride shotgun on the line's next run to Crow Canyon, on the other side of the Continental Divide, on Colorado's Western Slope. Because the owlhoots had tampered with the mail that the stage regularly carried, and had pilfered stocks as well as government bonds, the problem fell under the federal government's jurisdictional umbrella.

Longarm's assignment was to impersonate your average, cow-brained shotgun rider while investigating and, hopefully, running to ground the passel of at least seven men who'd been harassing the line, killing drivers and guards as well as innocent passengers. He wasn't sure how he'd do it—one man against a whole gang, whose numbers had been reported as anywhere between seven and fifteen—and from the driver's boot of a slow-moving coach no less. But the assignment was his, and Chief Marshal Billy Vail had had no spare men to send along to back his play.

"I'd imagine they do need a new guard," Rye said, as though she'd been reading the typewritten orders Longarm was carrying in an inside pocket of his corduroy jacket. "I heard that line's been pestered by highwaymen. That's all right—I'm not scared. They wouldn't hurt a girl, would they?"

"Can't see how they'd hurt one as pretty as you, Miss Rye." Longarm felt that thickness again in his throat as he studied the girl with bald admiration. From that gold-blond hair to the very tips of her moccasin boots, she was as easy on the eye as freshly spun honey.

"Why, thank you, Gus." Her pretty face acquired a beseeching look. "Am I pretty enough to impose on you to partner up with me tomorrow? I mean, let me tag along with you to Rabbit Ridge? It ain't the highwaymen I'm afraid of—it's that consarned Cormorant."

"I'd be pleased as pie to be so blessed with your company the rest of the ride to Rabbit Ridge, Miss Rye," Longarm said. "But are you sure ole Weed's dusting your backtrail? If he's employed by your father . . . ?"

"I don't doubt that he quit just to run me down. Or he might even have Pa's blessing in the matter. Either way, I've seen him doggin' my backtrail for certain sure. Him and him alone. I think I lost him yesterday going through that rocky stretch of desert north of Laramie, but I'll never feel totally free of that crazy, one-handed bastard till I'm safely in Bob's embrace!"

She was staring off toward the trail behind Longarm again, her brown eyes large and bright with fear. Her apprehension was catching, and Longarm found himself looking over his shoulder as well. The gunman she described, with a wooden hand and dressed in black, was like a nightmare specter from a child's imagination.

Longarm wasn't totally convinced the girl's own imagination hadn't gotten away from her. She seemed a little on the hot-blooded side. But he'd keep his eyes peeled and his ears pricked just the same.

He wanted no more surprises, no more delays on the way to Rabbit Ridge, where he had a job to take on.

He turned forward and caught the girl staring at him, the fear gone from her eyes, replaced by open admiration. She flushed a little, and then Longarm felt his own cheeks warm. He threw the last of his rye back, and tossed his cup on the ground.

"I'll tend the horses if you'll gather wood for a fire."

"Whatever you say, Gus," Rye said, throwing her own drink back.

She chuckled a little brazenly, the hooch now starting to hit her, and tossed her cup down to where it clinked against Longarm's. As she strode off through the brush, Longarm headed toward the grazing horses, catching himself glancing over his shoulder at the girl's delicious ass swaying inside her tight, doeskin shirt.

Chapter 4

Rye and Longarm, alias Gus Short, joined forces to build a fire and make supper. By the time they'd polished off the two roasted rabbits that Longarm had snared earlier in the day, when he'd stopped to water the bay, and the beans Rye had soaked in her coffeepot, good dark had closed down over the gorge.

Stars kindled brightly, and coyotes yammered in the surrounding ridges, sounding close enough to throw stones at.

"Oh, Gus, I'm a little worried," Rye said as she sagged down against her saddle, on the other side of the fire from Longarm. She held a cup of after-supper coffee in her hand as she tipped her hat back off her forehead to peruse the sparkling sky.

"Don't worry, Miss Rye," Longarm said. "My hearing's as keen as a hunting cat's, and I been called Hawk-Eye by more than one fella on more than two occasions. If ole Weed Cormorant decides to pay us a visit tonight, I'll hear him."

"No, it's not that." She sighed.

Longarm frowned as he added a drop of rye to his own steaming coffee cup. "What is it then?"

Rye sighed again and recrossed her ankles. "It's . . . well, I don't know how to put this without sounding like a harlot, but . . . I guess I'm kinda thinkin' it'd be fun to share your blankets tonight." She crumpled her face and turned her head this way and that in frustration. "And, gosh dang-it, I done promised myself I'd be true to Bob!"

Longarm cleared his heavy throat. "Well, Miss Rye . . . I think that's a right noble attitude. Last thing I'd wanna do is come between you and Bob."

She dipped her chin, setting one hand on the crown of her hat. Her blond curls partly obscured her face, across which the umber firelight danced.

"Don't you feel no pull toward me, Gus? No stirrin' of the old trouser snake?"

"Miss Rye, I feel plenty of stirrin'. And you goin' on about it isn't helpin' it any. Now, why don't you just resolve to keep your promise to old Bob, and I'll just resolve to sit here and sip my coffee in peace before pullin' my blankets up over my head for some nice, refreshing shut-eye."

Jesus, he thought. *This is torture. I never should have invited the girl to share my camp. I'm liable to start my undercover job in Rabbit Ridge with a weak ticker.*

"So . . . you feel it, too?" the girl asked hopefully.

Longarm chuckled without mirth and sipped his coffee.

"Well, I reckon that's good enough for me." Suddenly buoyant, Rye stood up and kicked out a place in the ground for her hip. Then she laid her blankets down, kicked out of her boots, and tossed her hat aside.

Plopping down on her butt, she stretched and yawned, her blouse drawing taut across her breasts. "Well, good night, Gus. Don't let the bedbugs bite, see you in the morning light!"

"Good night, Miss Rye."

She lay back, drew one of her blankets up over her legs, and turned onto her side, grinding her hip into the hole. Lifting her head suddenly, she frowned across the fire at Longarm.

"I'm a hot-blooded girl, and it bein' a warm night, I might decide later to shuck out of my clothes. If I do, I'll expect you to be a gentleman and keep your eyes closed, Gus."

"I make no promises, Miss Rye."

She stared at him, a wistful, coquettish look gradually shaping itself on her heart-shaped face, pulling up the corners of her rich mouth. She chuckled huskily and plopped back down, resting both her hands beneath her cheek against her saddle.

She squirmed around a little, grunting and groaning softly, but a minute hadn't passed before Longarm could hear her snoring softly beneath the pops and cracks of the fire.

Now it was Longarm's turn to chuckle, only he did it caustically. He was hard as a rock. Trying to let his mind drift into more sobering avenues like his current assignment, he sipped his coffee until he was sipping only grounds.

The grounds tasted like the delightful essence of rye.

He looked across the fire at Rye Spurlock. Her thick, blond curls had flopped down across her face, and her full breasts, pushing out the top wool blanket, rose and fell slowly as she breathed.

Longarm tossed his coffee dregs into the fire, got up, cursing under his breath, and grabbed his Winchester. He checked the horses where he'd tied them both to a short picket line where they could draw water and graze, then strolled downstream to get the lay of the night. When he'd walked a hundred yards, he walked upstream another hundred yards beyond the horses, neither hearing nor seeing any sign of the girl's alleged shadower or anyone else.

A wooden-handed half-breed named Weed Cormorant?

Longarm was beginning to wonder if Miss Rye Spurlock wasn't a little touched in the head.

When he walked back into the camp, he stopped suddenly. She lay staring up at him from his bedroll. In the glowing light of the campfire coals, he saw her smiling, showing her perfect white teeth. Her brown eyes twinkled faintly with reflected starlight.

Her hair was billowed out behind her. She held Longarm's top blanket across her breasts, revealing the bulging side of one, and nearly all of one creamy leg, which she'd turned to reveal the smooth inner thigh.

She said nothing, just lay there smiling.

Longarm, for his part, saw no reason to say anything either. Staring down at her, his heart quickening and his breath rattling in and out of his lungs, he set his rifle down calmly, and just as calmly kicked out of his boots and began shucking out of his clothes.

When he'd balled up his longhandles and tossed them away, he dropped to both knees over the girl. She sat up suddenly, holding the blanket over her breasts but not over much else.

"You don't think me craven, do you?" she asked.

Longarm ripped the blanket away from her chest and stared down at the two firm, swollen, pink-tipped orbs jutting toward him. "No more than me, Miss Rye."

He mashed his mouth against hers. Hers was open and waiting for him, her eyes squeezed shut.

Pushing her head back against the ground with his own, he positioned himself between her legs, his engorged, jutting organ throbbing so hard it ached. She reached down and grabbed him with her right hand, throwing her head back as she rubbed the swollen mushroom head of his cock against the furry, wet portal of her hot inner regions.

"Oh, sweet Jesus, Gus!" she gasped, running her fist up and down his aching length. "What a wonderful cock you have!" She poked the head of his shaft between her wet lower lips. "Go ahead, Gus—shove it in and take me for a long, hard ride. Bob and Cormorant and everyone else be *damned*!"

"Only if you insist, Miss Rye," Longarm grunted, lowering his hips to hers.

As she sucked air through her gritted teeth and dug her fingers into his shoulders, spreading her knees as wide as they would go and then some, he slid his manhood slowly inside her.

"Am I hurtin' you, Miss Rye?" he asked, as she locked her own arms around her calves and pulled her ankles back, groaning.

"If you stop, Gus," she wailed, "I'll cut your *heart* out!"

Longarm bottomed out inside her, he figured somewhere up north of her belly. He could feel her expanding and contracting wildly around him.

As he pulled his cock back to her opening, she bawled like a calf, and when he rammed himself back inside her again, she loosed another long, keening wail of exhaled air and dug her fingernails so deep into his shoulders that he thought that, in addition to a myriad of other sensations, he could feel the cool wetness of dribbling blood.

The bawling and wailing went on for a good, long time as Longarm gradually increased the speed of his pummeling of the delectable girl beneath him.

In and out, in and out . . .

"Oh, Gus! Oh, Gus!" the girl cried, her legs fairly beating like wings beside him as his hammering reached its zenith. "Oh, *Gawwwwwd,* you fuck good, Gus!"

At the end of his tether and propped above the writhing girl on his outstretched arms, Longarm slammed his groin against hers, held there, and stretched his lips back from his teeth. His seed shot into her like rapidly fired .45 slugs from a long, hot double-action shooting iron.

Every muscle in the girl's body grew taut. She threw her head up, hardening her jaws and squealing like a nymphomaniacal bobcat, clawing at the ground beside her and grinding her heels into Longarm's buttocks. As he spasmed against her, blowing his load, Longarm squeezed one of her breasts, feeling the pebbled nipple jutting against his palm.

When he'd finally finished, Longarm's own body slackened as did the girl's. She dropped her arms and legs, and Longarm collapsed on top of her, mashing his face between her warm, sweat-damp breasts. As her chest continued to rise and fall, slowing gradually, he could hear her heart beating against her breastbone. She ran her hands through his hair, caressed his legs with her feet, and sighed.

"I hope you haven't ruined me, Gus."

"How's that?" Longarm rasped.

"Bob doesn't fuck as good as you do."

Longarm swallowed, catching his breath. Their hearts were slowing in tandem. "Well, Miss Rye, there's more to happiness than . . ." Hearing the insincerity in his voice, he let the sentence trail off, punctuating it with a caustic chuff. No one enjoyed a good mattress or bedroll dance than Longarm. "Maybe he'll get the hang of it."

"I sure hope so," Rye said with a sigh, digging her fingers into Longarm's scalp, caressing the back of his neck with her fingers. Her nails raked him slightly, thrillingly.

Finally, he rolled over onto his back and stared at the glowing, frosty stars—so many that the Milky Way looked like smeared flour. Rye curled up against him, resting her head on his chest and playing absently with his cock and balls, running her fingertips lightly across his scrotum, up his cock, and back down again. After a few minutes of such ministrations, Longarm was beginning to grow hard once more—by Rye's design, he realized when, making little animal grunts, she slid her head down to his crotch and began tonguing him very gently so that only now and then could he feel the blissful sweetness of her tongue against the blossoming mushroom at the end of his cock.

Longarm lay like 180 pounds of melted butter. As the girl's head moved down around his crotch, he could hear only the fire's dying coals, the faint rustle of the breeze in the cottonwood branches, and the occasional rustling of burrowing creatures in the grass and dead leaves around him.

Occasionally, he became aware of his insistently thudding heart and the soft, wet sucking sounds of the girl bathing his cock with her own saliva.

After a time, when Longarm was as hard as he'd been before their first go-round, Rye got up and, in all her creamy, naked, beauty, breasts jostling beguilingly, tossed several logs on the fire. She knelt down, giving Longarm a thrilling view of her round rump and furred snatch from behind, and blew the flames alive.

When the fire was crackling and popping warmly, she got down on all fours—another sight that Longarm would remember on his deathbed—and shook her head like a frisky mare.

"Come on, Gus." She wagged her ass. "Once more, and then we can go to sleep and pretend nothing happened here but two weary pilgrims sharing the warmth of the same fire."

She giggled with delight.

Longarm chuckled. He was tired and sore from his roll and fall down the stone shelf and the dry snakebite, but he'd have had to be dead to turn down doing it doggie-style with such a delightful creature.

He mounted the girl from behind, and they quickly got down to business, Longarm snaking his arms under her chest to grab her breasts and, grabbing her thus, hammering her up and down on his cock. She'd been groaning and grunting, sagging and jerking before him, when she lifted her head suddenly to stare tensely off into the darkness beyond the flickering fire.

"What was that?"

Longarm had heard it, too. His Colt and cartridge belt were coiled nearby. Keeping his cock embedded in the girl's snatch, he slipped the .44 from its holster and fired three quick rounds toward the faint rustling and snorting sounds originating from straight ahead, about twenty yards out.

A faint mewling sounded, and then a low growl. Grass crackled under padded feet as the creature fled south through the trees.

Longarm tossed his Colt away.

"Coyote."

He grabbed the girl's hips once more, pushed her out to the end of his cock, then pulled her back down again, repeating the process until she was writhing and sighing in orgasmic bliss once more.

Chapter 5

In spite of his aches and pains and his carnal tussle with Rye Spurlock, Longarm managed a few hours of shut-eye before waking at the first flush of false dawn.

Somehow, he was able to stave off the lusty advances of the sexy, half-awake girl—one of the few beautiful women, he decided, who was also a shameless, indefatigable nymphomaniac. He was not only questioning whether Weed Cormorant was really after her, but whether the mysterious gunman even existed. Maybe she only fancied, out of some dark desire, that the black-clad, one-handed specter was fogging her backtrail. Possibly, Cormorant was only a figment of the girl's overactive, oversexed imagination.

When Longarm and Rye had eaten a quick cold breakfast of what remained of the rabbit and beans they'd had for supper, and washed it down with thick, black coffee, they saddled up and hit the trail for Rabbit Ridge.

If Rye was merely imagining that Cormorant was tracking her, her imagination was as strong as her sex drive, because she seemed thoroughly convinced it was true. She rode nearly constantly hipped around in her saddle, and when she wasn't staring down their backtrail, she was swing-ing her frightened gaze from right to left and back again, clamping both hands around her saddle horn.

Her anxiety was catching. Several times, Longarm rode a quarter mile back to make sure they weren't indeed being shadowed by a one-handed, black-clad man on a tall, cream horse—with pearl-gripped, silver-chased pistols, no less!—though every time he conjured the image he had to chuckle.

"You don't believe he's back there, do you?" Rye said when he'd returned from his third scout with, apparently, a dubious expression.

"Well, shit, Rye," he said a tad defensively, "I haven't seen any riders or even a dust plume all day. All I see is you lookin' like the devil's yellow-toothed hounds are nipping at your heels!"

"Give a man your body and he stops taking you serious."

"Now hold on a second. I ain't sure I *ever* took that story seriously. Think about it, girl." Longarm hooded his brows at her riding her buckskin off his right stirrup. "A black-clad pistolero with a phony hand and silver-chased hoglegs!"

"I know it sounds like something outta them dime nov-els and illustrated newspapers, but he's *real,* I tell you. And just because you can't glass him, Gus, don't mean he ain't back there. Don't be such a tinhorn! He probably sees you with me and he's holdin' back, waitin' to get me off alone where no one can hear me scream while he's hogtying and doin' God knows what else before he throws me over my own saddle and leads me back to Sapinero!"

The girl scanned a rocky, cedar-stippled hill right of the trail, and added in a dark tone, "You best keep your own eyes peeled, amigo. I wouldn't want him bushwhackin' you 'cause he sees you ridin' with me and gets jealous!"

Something rustled in the sage to the right of the trail.

She gave a start, and turned to see a jackrabbit scuttling low to the ground, working its black nose, before it disappeared behind a boulder. Rye turned forward with a heartfelt "Whew!"

Longarm snorted and continued riding alongside the edgy girl in incredulous silence, her nerves filing his own to such a fine edge that when the shabby little burg of Rabbit Ridge appeared in a broad, bowl-shaped valley before and below them, he heaved a sigh of genuine relief.

"You oughta be safe here," Longarm said as he and Rye heeled their mounts into trots along the narrow, chalky trail, heading down a long, gradual slope. "Old Cormorant won't try anything amongst the good folks of Rabbit Ridge."

"Good folks?" She laughed. "Har-har. They say the ones that are hound-dogging the express company are from around here, and a lot of the folks from town know who they are but don't say 'cause they're afraid they'll get their tongues cut out. Cowards! Cormorant told me once he can smell a yellow dog a mile off. Smells like mink spray. No, sir—he'd go ahead and do to me what he pleased."

She glanced at Longarm, furrowing a pretty, thin brow. "You gotta stick close to me, Gus."

Longarm grumbled, "Well, I reckon once we board the stage, I'll only be as far away as the driver's boot."

"That eases my heart, but we got all the rest of the day and evenin' before we pull out tomorrow morning. Cormorant can do a lot of damage in that much time."

The shabby sandstone or board-and-batten shacks of Rabbit Ridge began pushing up along both sides of the trail that was heading toward the town's main drag. The low western limestone ridge, vaguely rabbit-shaped, which likely gave the town its name, pushed a wedge of cool, purple shade over about half the town's rooftops.

A couple of motley curs ran out from trash-strewn alleys or from their sleeping quarters beneath boardwalks to bark and nip at the hocks of Longarm's and Rye's horses before swaggering off to other pursuits with a devilishly satisfied air.

"See the Crystal Theater there?" Rye said, glancing at a tall, unpainted frame structure standing on the broad street's left side. Leaning westward at such a pitch that it appeared ready to collapse with the next slight breeze, the building looked more like a mercantile or even a hotel than a theater. "A few years ago I decided I wanted to come up here and get a job as a play actress and dancer. Pa said he'd disown me and that only harlots took such jobs. Now, I wish I'd have done it. Couldn't be much worse off than I am now."

"Only you got Bob waitin' for you on the other side of the Continental Divide," Longarm reminded her.

"That's right," Rye said, with the air of picking herself up by the bootstraps. "I got Bob, and he's cuter'n a yearling colt with a speckled ass and bridle bells!"

"There you go."

"Thanks for helpin' me look on the bright side, Gus."

"Glad to be of help." Longarm saw the sign for the stage line office, and halted his horse in the middle of the street. He nodded at the hotel one door down from the theater. "Why don't you go on over and get yourself a room and a bath? I have to talk to my employer. Maybe see you later on this evening."

Rye hipped around in her saddle again to peruse their backtrail. Longarm found himself doing the same. There was nothing out there but blue sky and sage. A single, small dust devil danced and quickly died. No sign of the menacing Weed Cormorant or anyone else.

Rye looked at Longarm with concern, then tossed her

head toward the hotel—three stories of green-painted boards with a large false front announcing in gaudy mauve letters: THE PRICKLY PEAR HOTEL AND SALOON. "You gonna hole up over yonder?" she asked.

"Looks like it's the only nap shed in town."

"All right. I'll see ya, Gus." Tentatively, Rye reined her tired horse across the street, glancing back over her shoulder and warning, "Don't be surprised if you hear gunshots and screamin' in short order."

"I'll come a-runnin', Miss Rye."

"You might," she said grimly, facing away now as she headed over to the Prickly Pear, her horse wearily swishing its dusty tail. "And you might be too damn late . . ."

Longarm stared after the girl, not sure what to make of the sexy blonde. Was she as loony as a tree full of owls, as he suspected, or was there really a kill-crazy, black-clad, one-handed professional gunman on her tail?

The issue unresolved—he doubted it would ever be resolved until he saw Weed Cormorant in the flesh—Longarm reined the bay up the street to the tall, roughshod Clark & Kinney Great Divide Line offices sitting along the street's right side at nearly the far edge of town. Beyond lay only a couple of corrals and wagon and hay sheds, all sheathed in wiry shrubs and tumbleweeds, and an old, wheelless Concord coach that appeared to have been slouching there long enough to have become home to several generations of diamondbacks and black widow spiders.

Everything out there looked only half tended, but the dozen or so horses milling in the three corrals appeared fine-boned and robust. One clean-lined sorrel was getting its tail brushed out by a half-grown boy in bib overalls and floppy-brimmed black hat, while a tabby cat rolled friskily in the dust behind him.

Longarm tossed the bay's reins over the hitch rack fronting the shabby offices, and followed a sign with a painted
arrow in the shape of a pointing finger and with the words
F. CLINE MCCALLISTER, STATION MANAGER up a creaky stair-
way along the building's right exterior.

The stairs slanted precariously to the outside, so Longarm climbed along the left, grasping the rail on that side as
if it would hold him if the entire contraption suddenly
broke loose from the building's rotten wall, as it seemed
about to do at any second, and plunged to the sage-pocked
ground below.

There was an OPEN sign in the window of the door at the
top of the stairs, so Longarm went on in and closed the
door behind him. He found himself standing in the shadows
of a cluttered office furnished with an even more cluttered
rolltop desk, several sagging bookshelves, and plank tables
sagging under clothbound ledgers, with a map of Colorado
and Wyoming Territory on one wall and a potbelly stove
abutting another.

Several burlap bags marked U.S. MAIL were crouched
on either side of the door, letters spilling from their partly
open tops. One letter was so far out of its bag that Longarm could see that it was addressed in ornate purple script
to one Corporal Keith R. Blair at Fort Randall, Colorado,
from one Mrs. Augustus M. Blair of Cheyenne, Wyoming
Territory.

The room smelled musty and slightly rancid, and there
was the odor of a recently cooked meal. From the beaded
curtain over a doorway in the opposite wall, the sounds of a
man's low groans emanated, and what Longarm judged to
be a woman's rapturous sighs.

Longarm shifted his weight from one boot to the other
and cleared his throat. The man continued groaning, adding

a grunt now and then, like that of a man stepping naked into a snowmelt stream, and the woman continued to sigh and gasp softly. A cot whined beneath the weight of the two lovers.

"Ahem!" Longarm said. "Mr. F. Cline McCallister, that you back there? Your new shotgun rider's reporting for duty."

He couldn't help grinning as, beyond the beaded curtain, the woman gasped and the man groaned loudly, startled.

"Jesus H. Fuckin' Christ!" the man croaked, the cot creaking so loudly that, like the outside stairs, it sounded ready to crumble into slivers and sawdust.

Longarm couldn't help grinning again as, sagging into a Windsor chair near the rolltop desk, he dug a nickel cheroot from his shirt pocket, hiked a boot onto a knee, and scraped a stove match to life on his heel. Meanwhile, much grunting and sighing and shuffling emanated from the room beyond the beaded curtain.

A gray-haired old codger with tangled, bushy mutton-chops pushed through the curtain, his washed-out blue eyes bleary behind round spectacles perched crookedly on his long, pitted beak. He was carrying a worn pair of half boots in one hand; on his feet he wore only wash-worn socks, one of which licked out a good three inches beyond his toes.

"Damn fine way to appear for a job, young fella!" the man barked as the curtain clattered back into place behind him. He was stooped over, wincing and ramming one fist against the small of his back as though working hard to straighten himself. "What makes you think I'd employ someone with the manners of a damn barn rat?"

"Nothin' makes me think that," Longarm grunted, drawing a lungful of smoke and releasing it slowly through his nostrils. "But you're not employing me, Mr. McCallister." Longarm paused. "Uh . . . you are McCallister, ain't you?"

Sandy Public Library

"That's right," the man said, tucking his white cotton shirt into wrinkled wool trousers.

"As I was sayin', you're not employing me. I'm Custis Long, deputy U.S. badge toter. As per your main office's request of the First District Court presided over by my boss, Chief Marshal Billy Vail, I'm here to work for free until we can run to ground the owlhoots pestering your stage line."

Longarm waved smoke from the air in front of his face. "Unless that little matter's been cleared up over the past two weeks it's taken me to finish my last assignment and haul ass out here."

"Oh." McCallister, who appeared in his late fifties, early sixties, took on a chagrined look as, adjusting his blue wool vest and watch chain, he dropped his lace-up black half boots on the floor by the desk and eased down in the swivel chair in front of it. "You're the deputy they sent. Heard you was comin'. Wasn't sure when you'd get here."

"Hope I didn't intrude on nothin' important," Longarm said, removing the cheroot from his mouth and casting a wry glance toward the beaded curtain. Beyond it, a slender shadow moved, and the floor creaked and thudded lightly with the stirrings of someone getting dressed.

"No, no," the man said, flushing a little as he reached down to pull a boot on. "Me and my ticket agent was just goin' over last week's receipts."

As the man hunched in his chair to pull on his second boot, grunting with the effort, a figure pushed through the curtain with a noisy clatter of the jostling wood beads. Longarm nearly choked on cigar smoke as the woman moved into the room clad in only a shapeless gray skirt.

Above the skirt she wore only a necklace of fine, flat, irregularly shaped turquoise stones on a cheap white string.

The necklace curved down over as fine a pair of naked, brown, pink-tipped breasts as Longarm had ever seen.

Every bit as nice as Rye Spurlock's, only slightly larger and pointed with insouciantly upturned tips.

The woman, a lissome Indian in her early twenties, with molasses-colored, almond-shaped eyes, gave Longarm an oblique half smile as, pausing between the curtain and the outside door, she reached up to pull a sleeveless, frilly Mexican-style blouse over her head.

She kept her eyes on the tall lawman as the blouse dropped down to cover her breasts, though not her slender, smooth shoulders, which were the color of freshly varnished walnut. She flipped her waist-length, coal black hair out from under the blouse's lace-edged neck, then continued to the outside door, which she disappeared through in less time than it took Longarm to draw another breath and realize that his imagination hadn't merely conjured her improbably queenly image here in this shabby, fetid stage station office.

Longarm stared at the door for a moment, a wry smile quirking his lip. He could hear the girl pad down the groaning, barking stairs. Turning to McCallister, he tapped ashes from his cheroot onto the floor and rasped, "Your ticket agent?"

The station manager shrugged a shoulder. "She has sold tickets for me time or two. But, uh . . . that ain't her expertise." His hawkish, bony face acquired a constipated look. "You ain't gonna tell my wife, are you? Or my boss in Laramie? I don't know which one's more persnickety."

"Your secret's safe with me," Longarm said. "As long as you tell me where that Injun princess works. I take it she does work—besides sellin' stage tickets, I mean."

"At the oldest trade known to man." McCallister gave a mirthful snort. "You'll find her over to the Heifer Bell Parlor House behind the theater. Name's Arizona. She works the Prickly Pear on occasion, when it's slow over to the Heifer Bell."

The station agent laced his second shoe and pulled open a desk drawer. "The girl's about to give me a heart condition, but after thirty-five years of marriage to the same old hag, and a full quarter of those years working out here in the middle of fuckin' nowheres for the two old skinflints Clark and Kinney, I'm ready to be turned six feet under anyway. Those men are tighter'n the bark on a tree, and I'm so sick of dust and wind I could cry real tears. I grew up in New York City, fer chrissakes!"

He held up a bottle, and his right eye narrowed behind a thick spectacle lens as he glanced at Longarm's puffy cheek. "Looks like you run into a cur that wouldn't let go of your mug. Shot of giggle juice to cut the trail dust and kill the ache before we get down to brass tacks, Marshal?"

Chapter 6

Longarm and F. Cline McCallister each threw back a quick
shot of the busthead the station agent kept in his desk
drawer. McCallister refilled their glasses, then corked the
bottle and returned it to its resting place, kicking the drawer
closed with a grim sigh.

"Well, I sure do hope you can run these gunslicks to
ground, Deputy Long. Like I said, I been a station agent out
here for a good number of years—more than I like to think
about, in fact—and I don't recollect ever before having the
trouble these boys are causing. The boss over to Laramie
probably done told you that if these holdups keep up, we
ain't gonna get no more passengers fool enough to ride our
coaches, and the mine up to Talley ain't gonna be usin' us
fer bullion runs neither.

"If them two things happen, I'll be boardin' up this place
and lookin' for another job. And as much as I've grown
weary of residin' out here on this canker on the Devil's ass,
at my age I look with more than a little apprehension at my
prospects for finding employment as anything but a saloon
swamper!"

The station agent sagged back in his swivel chair and shook his head grimly.

"I didn't talk directly to your boss in Laramie," Longarm said, sipping the Who-hit-John like a man testing a spring for Apache-poisoned water. It was godawful stuff, but it did cut the trail dust and ease the trail-aggravated aches in his bones. It also quelled the heat in his puffed cheek. "I got all my information second- or third-hand from my own boss. It was all typed up pretty on the reports I got here in my coat pocket, and while I've perused the papers, there's nothing like getting the goods straight from the factory."

"Well, it's simple enough." McCallister leaned forward to daintily sip from his own glass before carefully setting the glass atop his desk, rising from his squawky chair, and moving over to the large map of Colorado and Wyoming Territory on the room's east wall. "The gang of thievin' cutthroats—who they are is anyone's guess, as no one aboard the hit stages has recognized 'em—have hit the run to Bull Hook Bottoms right here."

McCallister set a long, red, knobby finger on what appeared to be a winding stretch of canyon trail climbing toward the crest of the Continental Divide very near the border between Colorado and Wyoming Territory.

"There's a long, fifteen-mile gap through this barranca known as Demon Rock Canyon that's easy pickin's for a few men on horseback fixin' to run down a stage."

"I take it the trail's steep and slow."

"Near the pass it's very steep, and slower than a Lutheran church service. And we been hit in there, at a different place each time, four times over the past six months."

"And how many men in this party of owlhoots? Any handle on that yet?"

"The last driver hit counted around ten. Once there was

twelve. Hard-nosed, fork-tailed gunhands of the lowest mark, but damn good with shootin' irons. So far, they've killed two of our drivers, three passengers, and . . . uh . . . a goodly number of our shotgun messengers."

Longarm sipped his drink again, then leaned forward to set his own half-empty glass down beside McCallister's. He doffed his hat and ran a hand through his sweat-matted hair. "Well, that's as simple as a Sunday-mornin' hanging. I know where we're likely to get hit, give or take fifteen miles, and by how many border toughs, but my question is this, McCallister. You've been hit four times in the past six months. How do you know we're going to get hit on *this* run that *I've* been assigned to? I mean, I hate to think I might've come all the way out here on the taxpayers' money for nothin'."

"That's simple, too, Deputy Long. Every time we was hit, we was carrying gold bullion from the mine up at Talley to the Stockmen's Bank in Crow Canyon. That's prime beef country over thataway. Lots of rich stockmen with lots of cow nurses to pay each and every month."

"And you're hauling more this run."

"Give the man a cigar!" McCallister intoned without mockery. "We wasn't hit the last run, but we was hit the one before that. So, we're due. If they don't hit us in the next three days it takes you to get over the Divide, I'll stand on my head in the middle of Main Street on Sunday morning and sing 'Danny Boy' at the tops of my lungs!"

McCallister sagged back down in his chair and rested his shot glass on his thigh. "And if we lose another strongbox worth . . . oh, somewheres around fifty and sixty thousand dollars . . . it's curtains for the company. Curtains for me and the missus, I might add, though I ain't so worried about Bertha as I am for myself. That woman's got such a strong, sour disposition, she could survive on the moon with nothin' but a wool wrap and a pot of English tea!"

"Right likable-soundin' woman," Longarm quipped. "The stage from Talley's due in tomorrow, I take it?"

"Bright and early. You'll be rollin' out shortly there-after."

"Who's the driver?"

"Johnny Anderson." McCallister, apparently tired of nursing the coffin varnish, tossed the whole rest of his shot back, smacked his lips, and swabbed them and his thin mustache with his tongue. "He's probably over to the Prickly Pear right now, good an' drunk. Never seen a man stay so absolutely pie-eyed between stage runs, but as soon as he climbs aboard the old Concord, he don't touch a drop. I know 'cause I got spies."

"Good with a gun, this Anderson?"

"When sober, he could outshoot Buffalo Bill his ownself with a sixteen-shot Henry. That's what he carries. He was jayhooin' the last run that was held up, but they didn't give him a chance. Shot the shotgun messenger and were all over that stage like ugly on Mrs. McCallister her ownself!"

Longarm threw back his shot and slammed the glass on the desk. Standing, a grim cast to his brown eyes, he adjusted the .44 on his hip and turned to the door.

"Well, I reckon I'll head on over to the Prickly Pear and introduce myself to my colleague. He doesn't know I'm a federal badge toter, does he?"

McCallister shook his head. "No one knows that but you, me, and my boss in Laramie. I'm as tight-lipped as a church deacon with a fresh case of the pony drip."

Longarm extended his hand to the station agent. "Mr. McCallister, been a pleasure. Of course, under the circumstances, I'm exaggerating."

"Same here, Deputy Long."

"Call me Longarm."

"All right then," the station agent said, squawking up from his own chair and following Longarm to the door. "If I see ya alive and kicking again, I'll do that."

He reached in front of the lawman to open the door, then stopped abruptly. "Oh." He walked back to his desk and reached for something on the far side, then hefted a long, double-barreled shotgun in the air before him. It was a much-scarred old popper with tarnished barrels and a leather lanyard that doubled as a bandolier, the loops of which were filled with buckshot loads.

With a grunt, McCallister tossed the gun to Longarm, who caught it one-handed. "Don't forget this, shotgun man!"

Longarm breeched the savage-looking weapon. Both bores yawned empty. He could faintly smell old powder mixing with the cloying aroma of gun oil. Dust streaked the front and rear stock, and sand was crusted in the groove between the barrels. It hadn't been cleaned recently. Nor had it been fired.

"If'n you want more wads, the gunsmith Arney Hanson'll fix you up. Tell him to put 'em on the stage line's tab." McCallister smiled balefully. "Sad to say, I doubt you'll get a chance to use 'em, but it might make you feel better. . . ."

Snapping the heavy, eight-gauge weapon back together with a loud, metallic pop, Longarm said warily, "You said those killers done turned toe-down—and I believe this is a direct quote—'a good number' of shotgun guards. How many would that be exactly?"

McCallister lifted his eyes to the ceiling and sagely fingered one of his curly gray muttonchops. "Well, let's see— we been hit a total of four times. And each time, the shot-

gun guard got blasted out of his seat and straight to Kingdom Come before he even knew what hit him." The manager shot Longarm an ominous, death's-head grin. "So,
that'd be four."

"Every one, huh?"

"Every one."

Longarm scowled. His boss, Billy Vail, hadn't told him
that bit of grim news.

Pinching his hat brim at the station agent, he turned back
to the door. "Obliged."

"Not at all," McCallister said as Longarm started down
the hazardous stairs.

The kid at Wolfgang Langer's Livery and Feed Barn was a
skinny shaver, about thirteen, with longish sandy hair and a
nose that had apparently been broken and not set right, for
it had a hump across the bridge and it listed dramatically to
one side. The scar along the side was curved like the front
of a horse hoof.

As Longarm approached on his bay, the kid stopped
sponging mud from the right wheel of a high, leather-seated
buggy parked before the barn's open doors.

The soapy water from his sponge rained into the
manure- and straw-littered dirt beside his high-topped, lace-
up boots as he studied Longarm skeptically. "You the stage
line's new shotgun rider?"

"You got it," Longarm said as he swung down from the
saddle.

"Seen you pull your army bay over to the depot building." The kid glanced at the big double-bore coach gun
hanging by its bandolier lanyard from Longarm's saddle
horn. "Seen you come out with that sawed-off ball shredder."

"You don't miss much, do you, sonny?" Longarm hadn't figured on anyone noticing the brand on his army-issue mount. But then, kids notice everything. Next time, he'd have to talk his budget-strangled boss, Billy Vail, into renting one from a private dealer. "It so happens I acquired this horse fair and square, and I got the receipt to prove it," Longarm told the kid with an air of manufactured defensiveness.

"Don't get your neck up, mister. I don't care if you stole this horse from the governor his ownself. If you wanna leave him here while you haul ass over the Divide and back, it'll be two dollars a day, ten cents a day extra for cracked corn or oats."

"That come with a daily curry?"

"Nope. That's just to corral, feed, and water him. Someone has to haul the feed and water, you know, and I don't do it for free."

Longarm frowned down at the lad, whose head came only up as far as Longarm's third vest button. "You don't *own* this place, do you, sonny?"

"No, but I sure as hell look after it. And, if Mr. Langer keeps drinkin' himself silly before noon, I figure it'll be mine in no time, since ole Langer don't have no relatives and all and his liver's already big as a watermelon."

"Quite a businessman, aren't you?"

"Yessir."

"How much for the curry?"

"Twenty-five cents."

"A day?"

"Someone's gotta—"

"I know, I know," Longarm said, cutting the boy off. "Someone's gotta do the work, and that'd be you. I just wonder how much is actually going into Mr. Langer's pocket."

The kid just smiled, the breeze blowing his sandy hair about his faintly freckled forehead.

"If you was a little taller, I'd dicker you down to a free curry, but I was taught only to pick on folks my own size."

Longarm dug his wallet out of his inside coat pocket, plucked out a few bills, and handed them over to the kid, who grabbed them greedily with his dirty, sun-roasted, work-hardened little hands. The boy counted the money quickly, expertly.

"Oughta do it."

He shoved the bills in a back pocket of his baggy cover-alls, and grabbed the bay's reins. He glanced up at Longarm, toed the dirt, glanced away, then looked up at the tall lawman once more. "If'n, say . . . if'n you happen to run into a little trouble on that Concord's hurricane deck. . . ."

"Why, you hard-hearted little pup!"

"We all gotta prepare for the unexpected, mister!"

"Christ, you sell caskets on the side?" Longarm shook his head as he shouldered his saddlebags, then walked around his horse to free his rifle sheath.

He glanced at the kid, who stared up at him with wide-eyed expectance.

Longarm chuckled despite the gooseflesh he felt rising on the back of his neck, and clamped his sheathed rifle under his arm. Looping his shotgun over his shoulder, he grabbed his war bag and began stomping off toward the Prickly Pear Hotel & Saloon. "Don't you worry silly about me, little amigo," he grumbled. "I'll be back for the horse."

He wasn't sure—it could have been his imagination—but he thought he heard the kid snort as he led the bay into the barn, and mumble, "Don't count on it, mister."

Chapter 7

"COCK-A-DOODLE-DOOOOOOOO!"

Longarm, loaded down with gear, including the eight-gauge shotgun and his Winchester '73, stopped in the street before the Prickly Pear Hotel & Saloon. It was from one of the establishment's upper-story windows that the raucous bellow had originated.

A woman laughed heartily and said, "Johnny, it ain't mornin', you fool!"

The man's crazed, hooch-inspired bellow blasted out the window once more. "COCK-A-DOODLE-*DOOOOOO-EEEEEEE!*"

The whooping, laughing shriek was pitched even higher and louder than before, as though the man were trying to win a contest for the most obnoxious drunken reveler north of the Rio Grande, and set several dogs to barking.

Again, the girl laughed and chastised the man with words Longarm couldn't hear above the man's own guffaws. Standing in the street before the otherwise quiet hotel's broad front porch, the gear-laden lawman poked his hat brim off his forehead and looked up at the second and third stories.

It was impossible to tell in which room the man and the woman were frolicking, but the hoorawing seemed to originate from the second floor, just above the saloon.

Longarm glanced up and down the quiet street. There weren't many folks out and about this time of the day and in the middle of the work week. Most of the drovers were likely sticking close to their ranges. One shopkeeper was out sweeping his boardwalk, however. He glanced toward the hotel and saloon, then, continuing to sweep without missing a beat, shook his head in disgust.

Something told Longarm that the gent had heard the cacophony a few times before.

Still hearing the woman's voice good-naturedly cajoling the drunken reveler, who seemed to have vented most of the steam from his boilers for the time being, Longarm mounted the hotel's broad steps, crossed the porch, and pushed through the batwings.

He paused to get the lay of the place, as was his custom, having been a lawman for more years than he'd care to think about and having made his share of enemies. He might have been pretending to be a shotgun rider here in Rabbit Ridge, but there were more than a few men on the frontier who'd recognize him for who and what he was—and not hesitate in the least about slapping leather on him to avenge a past rebuke.

None of that here, however. The three men playing cards—a gambler in a gaudy checked suit and two rough-garbed cowboys—at a table down near the big mahogany bar at the back of the room gave Longarm a casual once-over, then resumed their game. They clapped cards and clinked coins and loosed cigarette and cigar smoke at the low, stamped-tin ceiling.

The two sitting up near the front—a young man in cavalry blues and wearing lieutenant's bars on his shoulders and, improbably, a young brunette who was apparently the man's wife—glanced at Longarm with even more dismissiveness as they huddled together at their table against the left wall, immersed in serious discussion.

The man and woman were no doubt stage passengers idling away the hours before boarding tomorrow and heading for one of the several Army outposts on the Western Slope in either Colorado or Wyoming. Odd for a woman of high breeding, which this woman was, judging by her brocaded green traveling outfit and felt, feathered hat that was perched atop her immaculately coifed brown hair, to be patronizing a crude saloon. But likely, she didn't want to stray too far from the safety of her dashing young husband and the Army Colt on his hip.

Doubtful she'd run into any of her society friends out here in the middle of dusty nowhere anyway.

As a roar of laughter sounded in the ceiling toward the rear of the room, the woman looked up with a sour expression on her pretty, pale features and said, *"Disgusting!"*

The beefy apron who'd been whistling softly behind the bar as he stacked freshly washed shot glasses into a neat pyramid, glanced at the woman, then moved down the bar a ways. He reached beneath the mahogany and pulled out a barn blaster of slightly smaller caliber than Longarm's eight-gauge, and rammed the butt against the ceiling above his head.

"Hey, Johnny!" he barked in a gravelly voice. "Hold it down up there, ya randy son of a bitch!"

The barman—barrel-chested, with an enormous hard gut pushing out his soiled cream apron—glanced at the lieutenant's woman and smiled with chagrin. "Pardon my French. We don't get too many . . . uh, *nice* ladies in here." He tossed his head to a door opening off the room's right wall, beneath a row of three horseshoes and a plank in which the word DINING had been burned. "Perhaps you'd be comfortable in the dining room over yonder."

"I'm fine here, Mr. Deerhorn, if you'll only encourage your male customers to mind their manners."

The two middle-aged cowboys and the slightly younger gambler paused in their game to glance at the woman wryly before continuing to toss around pasteboards and coins while filling the air with thick swirls of harsh-smelling tobacco smoke.

Longarm headed for a table near the dining room door. "Barkeep, I'll take a boilermaker," he yelled toward the front of the room. Then he tossed all his gear except for the barn blaster down beside his table, stepped over it, and plopped into a chair with his back facing the room's front corner.

Meanwhile, the barman filled a shot glass, dumped beer from a silver spigot, came around the mahogany with a drink held in each greasy hand, and set both on the table before Longarm. "My girl ain't in yet," he said with an indignant scowl.

Longarm flipped a silver piece into the air and raised the beer to his lips. "Figured you could use the exercise."

The barman snorted and turned away. Before he could take a step, Longarm said, "Say there, Mr. Deerhorn?"

The big man turned back, scowled down again at Longarm, his horsey, buck-toothed face framed by long, greasy, brown hair. "Yes?" he said with exaggerated servitude.

Longarm ran a hand across his longhorn mustache, feeling silly. "You ain't, uh, seen a tall, black-garbed man within the past hour or so, have you?"

The barman hiked a heavy shoulder. "There's Ramey Wells. He was in here a few—"

Longarm shook his head, cutting the man off. "This fella has a . . . well, a . . . wooden left hand. Mean-lookin' gent with silver guns and black holsters, probably a buscadero rig. Woulda rode in on a cream stallion."

Deerhorn narrowed a skeptical eye. "Tall, black-dressed rider on a cream stallion. With a wooden hand. If this is a joke, friend, get to the punch line, will ya? Don't got time to stand here and—"

"Never mind," Longarm said, again cutting the man off and sipping his beer, feeling a warmth in the tips of his ears.

"What's with the shotgun, amigo? Goin' bird huntin'?"

Longarm shook his head and licked the beer foam from his mustache. "Shotgun rider for the stage line."

"No shit?"

"None at all."

"Well," the barman said with a laugh, "don't expect to start a tab!"

"Can a dead man get a room?"

"Two dollars in advance."

Longarm tossed more silver in the air. The man caught it against his broad, shelving chest. "See me before you head upstairs and I'll give ya a key. If you want a last fuck, Miss Coffee's girls'll be over later."

He laughed and walked away.

Later, when Longarm had finished his boilermaker, he got his key from Deerhorn and hauled his gear up to his second-story room. He considered checking on Rye Spurlock, but nixed the idea. The poor girl was probably catching some much-needed shut-eye. He'd find out what room she was in and check on her later, make sure she hadn't been carted off by the formidable Weed Cormorant.

Since he had nothing better to do, the lawman headed back downstairs for another drink. Later, after a few more drinks and supper, he'd work his way into the poker game for something to do. Then he'd turn in early. It sounded like he was going to need his beauty sleep.

Or shotgun sleep.

Tomorrow, he wasn't only going to need eyes in the back of his head, but in his ears as well. And that might not even save him if the owlhoots haunting the stage line hid a sharpshooter a long way off the trail in some high rocks or a tree, say, and pinked him before he even had time to peel back the big popper's hammers.

"Shit, Billy," he said to himself, back at his table and sipping another beer. "You've sent me off on some dick-rippin' assignments before, but this one here sounds like a whole new wagonload of shit-stompin' trouble. One man against ten including a sharpshooter. I'm liable to get a blue whistler in the back of my head and not even hear the whistle."

Longarm had never feared any man. And he'd been outnumbered before. Badly outnumbered. But a man he couldn't see firing a bullet he might not even hear was a whole other thing.

Too late to do anything about it now, though. The only thing he could do was scour the trail ahead and behind and around the stage as well as he could, and hope his past sundry sins wouldn't come back to nip him in the ass.

The lieutenant and the lieutenant's pretty wife had gone into the dining room, and Longarm was considering joining the ongoing poker match, when the thumping and occasional laughter in the ceiling died. A few minutes later, boots thumped on the stairs at the back of the room to the right of the bar.

Longarm looked up over his whiskey glass and burning cigar to see a tall, potbellied man in a long, spruce green duster descending the stairs, a little wobbly on his feet and paying close attention to each step. His duster was thrown back behind a nondescript .44 holstered on his right hip, butt forward, and his black, sun-coppered Stetson was pulled down low over his eyes.

When the man reached the bottom of the stairs, he stopped, hitched up his pants and gunbelt, looked around the room, then went over to the bar for a bottle.

As Deerhorn filled the order, he tossed his head toward Longarm and said something Longarm couldn't hear. The duster-clad gent, whom Longarm assumed was the stage driver, Johnny Anderson, paid Deerhorn for the bottle, then, grabbing the bottle by the neck and one shotglass off Deerhorn's immaculate pyramid, clomped over to Longarm's table and stared down at the lawman grimly.

"That's right," Longarm growled. "I'm the dead man who'll be sharin' the driver's boot with you next run."

"At least it'll be quick."

"That's what I hear." Longarm kicked out a chair on the other side of the table. "Have a seat, 'less you're superstitious."

"No, hell. I been ridin' with dead men regular of late." The driver plopped his bottle and glass on the table and sank heavily into his chair. "Only, I didn't know it at the time. This makes me one up on the game."

"Gus Short."

"Nice to know you, Gus," the driver said, shaking Longarm's hand. "Johnny Anderson."

"Gathered." Longarm glanced at the ceiling. "You, uh, got a favorite up there?"

"All Miss Coffee's girls are my favorites. More'll be over later. You might find one yourself. Might as well enjoy yourself whilst you can."

Anderson splashed whiskey into his glass, then reached over to refill Longarm's. "It ain't—you know—too late to turn tail and run like a donkey with its tail on fire. Personally, I wouldn't ride on the right side of the boot for all the girls in Miss Coffee's parlor, and she's got some right nice ones. And I wouldn't think any less of you."

"That's only 'cause you don't think anything of me, not knowin' me an' all."

Anderson lifted his glass in salute. "Too-shay."

Longarm sipped his whiskey, then sank back in his chair. He drew deeply on his cigar, then blew the smoke over the bearded head of the stage driver—a man in his mid-to-late fifties, judging by the deep lines around Anderson's eyes and in his sunburned cheeks above his scraggly beard.

"Well, you got as good a look at them killers as anyone," Longarm said. "You got any idea who they are?"

Anderson shrugged. "All I know is there's nine or ten of 'em, maybe eleven, and they don't take no shit from nobody. They come in fast as loco mustangs—after they've turned my driver toe-down, that is—and if all the passengers and me included don't move as fast as they like, givin' up our personals, they shoot. And they shoot to kill."

"Professionals?"

Anderson nodded. "Sure as shit. Pros by experience. Like I said, there's damn near a dozen. Leader's a short guy with a pink neckerchief—don't even come up to my Adam's apple. Nasty son of a bitch, too. Close-set eyes and a long beard, deerskin leggings. First time they pulled down on us, he and another man he called his brother and a blond gent with a nasty scar above his eye hauled a couple girls off and raped 'em. I heard one o' them girls ain't been right in the head since."

"Which one kills the poor shotgun guard?"

"A young pup with a bowler hat and a Sharps Big Fifty. Flat eyes. Never says anything, just grins. Treats that rifle like it's his third arm, and his favorite one at that. Musta growed up huntin' buffalo or rustlers or some such."

"Tripod?"

"He always has one hangin' off his horse. So, yeah, that's what he uses all right. Gives him a damn steady shot. *Boom!* And I turn to see the shotgunner's brains dribbling out his forehead or one of his ears just before he rolls forward out of the boot or slithers down the side like fresh cow plop."

"Here's to tomorrow," Longarm said, raising his shotglass.

Anderson whooped and clinked his glass against his new shotgunner's. *"Tomorrow . . . if none thereafter!"*

Chapter 8

"Hello there, shotgun man," the woman in the hall said. "I was wondering if you really wanted to fuck me as much as I thought you did when I saw you at McCallister's."

Longarm blinked sleepily as he stared at the black-haired woman through the partly open door of his hotel room. He wasn't sure what time it was. He'd turned in after supping with the jehu, Johnny Anderson, and after playing several rounds of two-handed stud with the cheating old stage-driving cuss.

When the woman had knocked on his door, he'd been dead asleep, but he could still hear a din rising from the saloon downstairs, where a dozen or so more drinkers and cardplayers had gathered earlier that evening. They were mostly shop owners from Rabbit Ridge, with a few cowboys and drifters thrown into the fray as well.

It was probably only a little after midnight.

"You ain't shy, are ye?" Longarm asked.

"Uh-uh." The woman shook her head, her long black hair hanging straight down her shoulders. Her brown eyes flashed in the light from the hall's red-chimneyed lanterns. "Didn't take you for the shy type neither."

"How'd you know where to find me?"

"Johnny."

"Funny Johnny didn't take you himself."

"Johnny can't afford me."

"What makes you think I can?"

"Because I'm not charging you."

Longarm wrinkled a brow.

The woman laughed huskily. She had a sexy, raspy voice, like the gradual breakup of a frozen mountain stream. It was slightly Spanish-accented. "Can I come in, or would you like to do it out here in the hall? I'm not particular where I do it, when I'm doing it with the right man."

Longarm stumbled back into the room, his heart thudding slow and heavy against his breastbone. He drew the door wide and tossed his .44, which he'd grabbed from its holster when he'd heard the tap on the door, onto the dresser. As the girl shuffled in behind him and closed the door softly, he fumbled around until he got a gas lamp lit. Returning the chimney to the lamp, he turned to the girl, who was standing a few feet in front of the threshold.

His heart thudded. His throat contracted and expanded, intermittently squeezing off his wind.

She stood holding her arms behind her back, chin up, proudly displaying the ripe, tan breasts that were tauntingly visible through her black mesh blouse. Below the blouse—if you could call it that; it was more like fancy chicken wire or a swatch of a fishing net—billowy, black pajamas covered her long, lithe legs, trimmed with flashing gold sequins. The pajamas dropped as far as her ankles, revealing her fine-boned, lightly tanned feet, the nails of which were painted light pink.

Longarm's gaze swept back up to her breasts. Her nipples caressed the mesh, pointed ever so slightly outward and upward. They appeared about half erect. Her breasts rose and fell slowly, heavily, as she breathed. In the lantern light, the mesh laid delicate shadows across the smooth, tan skin of those full, firm orbs.

Longarm chuckled. "You sure as shit couldn't be desperate enough to be giving that away for free."

"I'm not giving it away for free, Mr. Short," she said in that raspy voice that only enriched Longarm's primal desires and set his ears to humming softly. "I'm here for satisfaction." She stepped toward him. "Do you know how long it's been since I've been satisfied? I mean *really* satisfied, the way a woman deserves now and then, just as a man does?"

Longarm stepped toward her, slid her hair back away from her cheeks with the backs of his hands, lightly rested his arms on her shoulders. Large silver hoops dangled from her ears. "Long time, I take it?"

"A long, long time."

"What makes you think I'd be any different?"

She glanced down. Longarm felt a coolness at the end of his cock, and he realized his erection had found its way out of the button fly in his longhandles. Still looking down at the swollen head of his shaft gently prodding her belly button, she said, barely loudly enough for him to hear, "Women know these things."

Slowly, she slid her hands down between her and Longarm. She eased the rest of his cock out of his longhandles, then caressed it with her smooth, warm fingers.

"Just as I thought," she rasped, watching her hands toy with his shaft, her breasts rising and falling even more heavily now behind the shaded mesh. "You are much man, Mr. Short. And so inappropriately named."

"Call me Gus," Longarm croaked, his blood rushing to his head.

Her fingers were like little javelins of pleasure. They seemed to know exactly which parts of the male organ were the most sensitive, and they manipulated those places with the deftness of an expert pianist. The back of Longarm's legs trembled.

He ran his fingers across her lips and over her chin, which was ever so slightly dimpled.

"And I should call you . . . ?"

"Arizona."

"Ah, yes, Arizona," he whispered, running his fingers down the long, smooth length of her almond-colored neck. "Never heard of a girl called Arizona." With his right index finger, he traced the deep valley between her breasts over the thin strands of the mesh. "Know one called Georgia. Another Virginia. Even a Kentucky Jane and a Dakota Rose. Never an Arizona. But, damn"—he circled her right nipple with his finger—"I like it."

Continuing to deftly manipulate him with her fingertips, she leaned forward and rose on her tiptoes to plant a soft kiss on his chin. Her breath was warm and moist against his skin. "You're not only going to like my name, Gus. You're going to like how well I fuck you, too."

He placed both hands on her breasts, cupping them, caressing the nipples with his thumbs. "I don't doubt it a bit, Arizona. What's more, I think you're gonna like the way I throw the blocks to you, too."

She closed her entire hand around his dong, and squeezed almost too hard as she ran her tongue along his jawline, muttering, "I don't doubt it a bit, Gus."

"Now, then," he said, suddenly planting his hands under her arms and lifting her onto the edge of the dresser. She gasped in delight. "Why don't we get down to brass tacks?"

He tucked his fingers behind the waistband of her silk pajamas, and tugged them down her thighs. In a second, they were on the floor at his feet. She hadn't been wearing anything beneath them, and her long, tan legs curved down in front of him.

She squirmed around, shifting her weight, opening and closing her thighs. Her snatch was dark, some alluring pink skin glistening between the swirls of black hair in the flickering glow of the lantern. He could hear her breathing. Behind the black mesh, her breasts rose and fell with more and more fervor.

Longarm shoved his longhandles down to his ankles, and kicked them away. His engorged dong jutted in front of him as he moved toward Arizona, who wedged her heels against the front of the dresser and spread her knees as wide as they'd go.

He leaned into her.

At the same time that his mouth found hers, his cock found her open snatch and slipped inside, her pubic hair raking him gently. They entangled their tongues as Longarm took one more small step toward the dresser, and then the girl opened her mouth wide and made a throaty gasping sound as his rod hit bottom.

He winced, his lips still mashed against hers, as she dug her fingers into his biceps and wrapped her legs around his waist. She was stronger than she looked, and for a moment he felt as though he were being engulfed by a boa constrictor. She held him there against her, fully inside her, digging her fingers and heels into his flesh, shuddering, groaning deep down in her throat.

Then she eased the tension in her limbs, and he slid slowly back, kissing her savagely as she kissed him just as savagely back. He rammed into her once more. The back of the dresser smacked the wall with a heavy thud.

He pulled out, slammed in.

Thud!

Out, in, *thud!*

Out, in, *thud!*

Out, in, *thud!*

"Hey, what the fuck's goin' on over there?" a man shouted from a room across the hall.

Out, in, *thud!*

Another voice shouted from another room across the hall. "Hey, hold it down—will ya?"

"Ay, Dios mio!" Arizona screeched, clutching at him as though to a life raft.

Out, in, *thud!*

Longarm was hammering faster now, plundering the girl's steamy, expanding and contracting core. He was so enmeshed in his primal chore, clutching the edge of the dresser for leverage and pulling his head away from hers every now and then to see her rapturously twisted face and bouncing breasts, that he was only vaguely aware of the dresser's loud hammering on the wall, and the growing shouts and admonishing barks all around him.

From downstairs, he could hear delighted guffaws— probably those of Johnny Anderson, who'd known where Arizona had been headed.

The shouts slowly died as Longarm finished.

Silence returned to the hotel as, slick with sweat, Longarm slid the girl off the dresser. She clung to him, slumped, eyes closed, hair in her face, still breathing heavily and groaning as though she'd been impaled with a half dozen Apache arrows.

For a few seconds after he'd dropped her on his bed, he thought she'd stopped breathing. Then she opened her smoky, dreamy eyes. She smiled wanly. Slowly lifting her arms, she reached toward him as though each limb weighed ten pounds.

She opened her hands, extended her fingers.

Longarm raked his eyes across her long, willowy, bosomy body stretched out beneath him. Tan and wet, hair in her eyes, she closed her knees together and tipped them out of the way.

"Come," she groaned, smiling. "Hold Arizona gently for a while. You damn near killed me, you son of a bitch."

Longarm did as she'd urged, and they lay together, Longarm spooning against the woman from behind, for a long time. They slept for part of that time, waking from their dozing to fondle and caress and nibble and pinch.

Longarm cupped her breasts behind the intoxicating mesh fabric, massaging the full, firm, up-tilting orbs, suckling them. Somewhere long after midnight, after the hotel, including the saloon below, had become quiet as a church on Halloween, Arizona reached over her hip, grabbed his erection, and slid it into her snatch from behind.

They fucked very slowly, lying on their sides, spooned together and hot with desire, slick with sweat.

At length, Arizona propped herself on an elbow, cupping her cheek in her hand. She groaned softly as Longarm slid in and out of her from behind, lifting her chin and drawing air between her gently gritted teeth. Occasionally, she dropped her hand between them to caress his slowly pistoning member, slick with both their bodily fluids.

As their blood temperature began to climb to the boiling point, Arizona rolled onto her belly.

Keeping himself inside her, Longarm crawled between her legs and, kneeling, kept hammering away at her until she rose up on her own knees and grabbed the headboard in front of her. She thrust her wet, round ass in the air and lowered her head, groaning louder now as her arousal became more poignant.

"Oh, Jesus. Oh, the sweetness of Mother Mary. You're killing me, Mr. Short. I've never known such bliss."

Clutching the woman's hips, drawing her butt toward him as he thrust against her, Longarm quickened his pace.

From the hall, a floorboard groaned.

Longarm glanced at the door ahead and to the left. The crack at the bottom was black.

Another creak sounded, slightly higher-pitched than Arizona's groaning and the sighing of the leather bedsprings.

Longarm continued to gradually increase his pace as he kept one eye peeled on the crack beneath the door. Since the hall lamps had obviously been extinguished, he couldn't tell for sure, but he thought he saw a shadow move on the other side of the door.

His cock slid in and out of Arizona's sopping snatch, the girl beginning to bellow now as she twisted the spools of the headboard in her hands like prison bars she was trying to loosen. As his own blood began to bubble and smoke in his veins, Longarm reached for the big, double-bore coach gun leaning against the head of the bed.

"Oh," Arizona groaned, throwing her head back on her shoulders. "Oh! Oh! Oh!"

Longarm heard another creak in the hall, and the ring of what could only be a boot spur.

"Yes," Arizona sobbed.

Longarm raised the shotgun in both hands. He'd loaded the barn blaster just before he'd come to bed, as an unloaded gun was as useless as a dead horse or a comatose whore.

He thrust his hips quickly, back and forth. Arizona rocked before him, sweat beads glistening on her tan back.

"Oh, Jesus, yes, yes, yes!" she cried, shaking her head as though against an unendurable pain.

Longarm felt his seed begin to gush up from his balls.

At the same time, the door burst inward.

The entire room shook as splinters sprayed in all directions and the iron latch clattered across the floor and under the bed. Yelling at the tops of his lungs, a short, stocky gent in a wool plaid shirt bounded into the room, holding a Colt Sheriff's model pistol in each hand.

He was a round-faced gent with a shaggy goat beard. As he bellowed, eyes pinched nearly shut, he raised both pistols and swung toward the bed.

Arizona lifted her head as far as it would go, and screamed.

Longarm tripped the shotgun's left trigger. The thundering roar filled the entire room and rocked the walls.

KA-BOOMMMMMMMM!

The eight-gauge, double-aught buckshot clubbed the would-be assassin in the middle of his shirt, lifting him straight out of his boots. He wailed as the steel shot knocked him ass over teakettle, his socks hanging off his feet, both boots flying straight up in the air. His arms flew toward the ceiling, and both pistols popped at the same time, the .45-caliber bullets plunking into the ceiling over the bed.

Longarm caught a glimpse of another man behind the first—just before the first smashed back into the second, who yelped and hit the hall floor on his back.

Longarm heard himself bellowing and looked down to see his hips spasming against Arizona in the final throws of his eruption. The girl was keening like a tortured squaw, head turned to stare at the sudden carnage in the open doorway. She bounced on her knees, wagging her ass up and down, as Longarm's jism blasted her core.

Holding the heavy barn blaster in one hand, Longarm pushed the still-spasming girl away and down, his already dwindling shaft bouncing free.

"Ay, mi Dios!" Arizona cried in a chaotic mix of rapture and horror, scrambling onto her knees and clinging with one hand to the headboard as though to the rail of a sinking ship. *"Qué está sucediendo, Señor Gus?"*

"Don't exactly know what's goin' on here, Arizona." Longarm planted both feet on the floor and raised the smoking gut shredder toward the man scrambling out from under the one who'd been first through the door and had incurred a pumpkin-sized hole in the chest for his efforts.

The second man gained his knees. He was thinner than the first, but it was hard to make out his features, as the first man had smashed the second man's nose flat against his face when Longarm had blown the first man back out the door.

The second man wailed and blew blood from his lips as he raised one of his two pistols.

Naked and not the least self-conscious about it, Longarm straddled the dead man and aimed the shotgun from his hip. "Hold it, there, you drygulchin' bastard!"

He wanted the man alive. He couldn't find out from a corpse who'd sent him and his sidekick on their night-stalking kill mission.

Bellowing, his face looking like someone had smashed it dead center with a large, ripe tomato, the second man slid one of his pistols toward Longarm. Longarm had no choice but to trip the shotgun's second trigger.

The gunman's head disappeared in a frothy spray of blood, bone, and brain matter that the double-aught buck embedded in the wall behind the quivering shoulders from which a thick fountain of liver-colored blood geysered, painting the ceiling.

Longarm cursed and lowered the smoking head vaporizer. He turned to Arizona, still cowering atop the bed, her breasts sloping toward the mussed, damp sheets beneath her. She stared at Longarm, aghast.

Her nipples were still erect. Chicken flesh shone on her shoulders and down her arms. She shook like a kitten in a snowstorm.

"Well, Arizona," the lawman said, resting the double-bore on his naked shoulder. "If that don't grease your wheel hubs, nothin's gonna."

Chapter 9

The thunder of the coach gun and the screams of the men as they died in a hail of double-aught buck and geysering blood attracted nearly every bleary-eyed, formerly asleep hotel patron, including Johnny Anderson and the gent who owned the place and who, clad in a tattered green robe and long, soiled night sock, promptly lost his supper when he saw the slough of blood and viscera on the floor of his second-story hall.

Normally, Longarm would have flashed his badge at the local badge toter. But since he was on undercover assignment and didn't want anyone, including the Rabbit Ridge constable, to know who he really was, he tried to look as flabbergasted and innocent as possible. Gus Short was just the poor, hapless son of a bitch who'd come to town to take the shotgunner job with the stage line and who two well-armed brigands had tried to grease for mysterious reasons while old Gus enjoyed the company of the town's most comely sporting girl.

He had no idea who the gents were or why they'd tried to turn him toe down, but God as his witness, he was only using McCallister's coach gun to defend himself and the girl!

Arizona backed him up from her casual perch in a spool-back chair at the carnage's periphery, wearing only Longarm's shirt, her long, penny-colored legs crossed, idly shaking her foot. She smoked one of Longarm's cheroots and sipped a whiskey shot.

Meanwhile, the town constable, Milford Towback, tugged on his gray mustache while he inspected the blood and what was left of the bushwhackers. Seemingly satisfied with Longarm's story, and pronouncing that his investigation into the dead men's identities would resume in the morning, Towback hitched his pants up his skinny hips, shook his head darkly, and left.

When the hotel owner had apologized to the rest of his guests for the ghastly interruption to their night's slumber, and sent for two lackeys "to clean up this unsightly mess," Longarm donned his corduroy jacket since Arizona was wearing his shirt, and excused himself from the whore, who seemed in no hurry to leave in spite of the stench of blood. He tramped off, stocking-footed, to Rye Spurlock's room.

Rye had been the only guest of the six in the place who hadn't come to investigate the source of the tooth-gnashing din.

Longarm tapped on her door, hearing only the latching and locking of doors up and down the hall around him and a couple in the hall above.

He said softly, "Rye? Open up—it's Gus."

Still nothing. Longarm's blood quickened.

He'd just wrapped his hand around the walnut grips of his Colt, which he'd stuffed down behind the waistband of his trousers, when the latch clicked. The door opened a crack. A pretty brown eye stared out, cast with fear.

"Gus?"

"Yeah, it's me. I was just checking on you. It was too late when I came up to go to bed—afraid I'd wake you."

She opened the door twice as wide as before, but it still wasn't open a foot. "What was the shooting?"

"Wish I knew. Mind if I come in for a second?"

She pulled the door halfway open, grabbed his arm, and drew him inside. She wore only pantaloons and a camisole. She had her big bowie in her right hand.

Quickly, she poked her head into the hall and looked both ways before just as quickly closing the door and latching it quietly, wincing slightly when the bolt clicked home.

"He's here," she whispered, turning to Longarm.

"Who?" he said automatically, knowing the answer.

"Who do you think?"

"Cormorant?"

Rye nodded.

"How do you know?"

"I heard him in the hall several hours ago. Been too scared to leave my room since."

"You saw him?"

Rye shook her head. "I heard him, though. He drags one foot. And I heard him in the hall outside my door, draggin' that foot real slow and spookylike."

Longarm glowered skeptically. "He's got a wooden hand *and* limp?"

Rye nodded. "And he's here in Rabbit Ridge. Might be stayin' at this very hotel, Gus." She grabbed Longarm's wrist and stared up at him with beseeching eyes. "He knows I'm here, just doesn't know what room I'm in. Oh, you gotta help me, Gus. He'll try to nab me in the mornin' before I can make it to the stagecoach!"

Longarm raked a hand across the day-old stubble on his

jaw. A wooden hand and a limp to go with the rest of Cormorant's specterlike visage. His growing skepticism about the girl's story must have shown on his face.

"You don't believe me, do you. You think I'm makin' the whole thing up. You don't think he really exists, do you."

Whether the black-clad gunman existed or not, the girl obviously *thought* he did. If that's how it was, she was crazier than a moon-touched mare. All Longarm knew was that he hadn't seen the man downstairs earlier, and a man like Cormorant would stick out anywhere like a pink hog in a church pew.

"I ain't sayin' that, Miss Rye," Longarm said.

She crossed her arms on her breasts, cocked a foot, and scowled. "But you're thinkin' it."

"Never mind what I'm thinkin'. Here's what we'll do. You keep your door locked and don't step outside your room till I come for you in the mornin'. We'll take breakfast downstairs together, and then I'll escort you over to the stagecoach. If Cormorant tries to nab you, he'll have to go through me. And I'll be carryin' a mighty big doublebarreled coach gun."

Longarm took the girl's shoulders in his hands and stared down at her reassuringly. "Any man'd be a fool to go up against one of those."

She touched his hand. "Maybe you could stay with me tonight—you and your big gun . . . ?"

Longarm hesitated. He had Arizona in his own room, and Rye in here. Between the two, he was liable to get no sleep at all.

"I don't think that'd be a good idea, Miss Rye. Wouldn't want folks to think you're a loose woman now, would you?"

"I don't care."

"I care, Miss Rye. Besides, you'll be fine as long as you lock the door. I'll be right down the hall and around the corner. And I'm a light sleeper. If I hear so much as a mouse scratch at your door, I'll come a-runnin' with that big thunder gun."

Rye turned the corners of her mouth down. "All right. But if I hear that limp again, I'm gonna scream at the tops of my lungs!"

"You do that."

With that, Longarm kissed the girl's forehead and went out. Hearing her twist the key in the lock behind him, then prop a chair beneath the door, he headed back toward his own room, stepping carefully around the giant blood pool. Someone had hauled the bodies off, but there was enough brain- and bone-peppered blood in front of Longarm's door—and on the walls and ceiling around it—to keep a couple of swampers with scrub brushes busy for hours.

He pushed the door open to find the room empty. All that remained of Arizona was her musky fragrance, her cheroot butt in her empty shot glass, and Longarm's shirt hanging over the spool-back chair in the corner.

That was all right. He'd had enough cavorting for one night, and Arizona had probably been driven out by the smell of death in the hall.

He shed his jacket, pants, six-gun, and hat. He took a shot of Maryland rye straight from the bottle, stole a couple puffs off a half-smoked cheroot, propped a chair under the ruined door, and crawled into bed.

His nerves sizzled like lightning-struck tree branches. The night's violence—as well as the frisky frolic with Arizona—had left him with too much snap and pop. His pulse thudded in his temples.

But the seasoned lawdog had been fucked and bush-whacked before, though possibly not at the same time. Anyway, he had the uncanny ability to empty his mind at will.

After only a couple of futile minutes wondering who in hell his would-be assassins had been—old enemies or members of the wolf pack preying on the stage line?—he closed his eyes and drifted into slumber land at long last.

At six o'clock the next morning, having been awakened by the scrub brushes of two young Indian boys working on the blood in the hall outside his room, Longarm knocked on Rye Spurlock's door.

Silence.

"Rye?"

Silence. On the other side of the door there wasn't even the creak of a floorboard. Only the distant clatter of pots and pans in the kitchen downstairs.

Growing testy, Longarm cleared his throat loudly. "Rye? It's Gus. Open the fuckin' door."

The door latch clicked. Rye's face appeared in the two-foot crack. She was fully dressed in her calico blouse, doe-skin skirt, and moccasins, and she didn't look like she'd slept a wink. Her face was gaunt, her eyes were glassy, and her hair was matted in spite of what appeared to be a rushed brushing.

"You don't have to use barn talk. I had to make sure it was you. Cormorant can disguise his voice."

Longarm sighed and adjusted the gear, including the big shotgun, on his shoulders. "Mighty talented hombre, Cormorant."

"Sneaky is more the word."

Rye donned her hat, letting the braided rawhide chin

thong hang down against her amply filled blouse. She hiked her foot on a chair, lifted her skirt, and slipped her big bowie into the sheath strapped to her calf outside her moccasin.

"Have you looked around to make sure the coast is clear?" she asked.

Longarm hadn't, but he was growing more and more certain the coast was clear and that this beautiful, brown-eyed blonde had more than a few bats in her belfry. No point in arguing, though. He'd known crazy folks, and it was easiest just to play along with their craziness. If they said, "Look at that blue-skinned man with the red horns tumbling out of the clouds," you'd best reply with something like, "Yeah, look at that. It'd sure help if he had wings!"

"Coast is clear, Miss Rye. I've had me a real good look around."

"All right then—if you're sure."

She followed him into the hall, carrying a leather grip in one hand, a carpetbag in the other. "But you best keep that cannon of yours ready. He could jump out and grab me at any moment, and he'll likely try to shoot you to get you out of the way."

"Well, that'd do it, I reckon."

As they descended the narrow stairs to the saloon hall in the misty shadows of early morning, she looked at him, one brow arched. "You think I'm touched."

"I'm withholding judgment," Longarm lied.

"You do that," Rye said, as they reached the big, empty saloon hall, where all the chairs had been overturned atop the tables.

They headed toward the dining room, Rye looking around as though expecting Weed Cormorant to jump out from under one of the tables or from behind the bar. "But you won't be withholding it for long," she added.

All through breakfast, Rye continued to look cautiously around her. Whenever one of the guests drifted in from upstairs, she gave a little gasp and turned to the door, often placing a hand on her chest as though to quell her hammering heart.

"Damn shame," Longarm thought, sipping his coffee after polishing off his bacon and eggs, "for one so pretty and young to be rowing with only one oar."

Not that he was completely convinced that Weed Cormorant was nothing more than a figment of her doughy head, but he had a pretty good feeling that if the man was real, Longarm would have seen him—or seen sign of him—by now. Just the same, he'd keep one eye peeled for Cormorant, and the other eye—and all his other senses—attuned to trouble from the stage-robbing gun wolves.

Damn, he thought, ushering Rye out of the dining room. This was turning into an assignment for the entire U.S. Cavalry—not just one lone badge-toting federal with a crazy girl on his arm.

Outside the Prickly Pear, Longarm stopped and gazed across the street at the dusty red and yellow-trimmed Concord coach sitting before the stage depot. Three hostlers were hitching up the six-horse team while Johnny Anderson and the station agent, McCallister, stood gassing near the rear luggage boot. Overfilled mail pouches were humped at the station agent's feet.

The two drovers and the gambler whom Longarm had seen in the saloon the night before sat or stood around a rain barrel, smoking. He'd seen all three in the hotel dining room earlier. They'd become friendly with each other, the way travelers often did.

The dashing cavalry lieutenant and his attractive wife had still been drinking coffee when Longarm and Rye had left. The lieutenant had been in the hall last night after the shooting, looking dashing even at two thirty in the morning, even in a shabby gray-checked robe and worn socks. He'd also looked faintly gaunt and pale, though if he'd seen much action at all, he'd likely seen worse carnage than that out on the Indian battlegrounds.

Wisely, his pretty wife had remained in her room.

"Looks like we got about ten minutes before we pull out," Longarm said to Rye. "I'll get you aboard the stage, and then I'm gonna head on over to the gun shop."

He wanted to load up on ammo for the coach gun, in case he got a chance to use it.

Rye clutched his arm as she cast her frightened gaze up and down the street, which the rising sun was just beginning to touch with streaks and prisms of gold. "No, I'll go with you!"

Longarm sighed. "All right then."

Stepping off the boardwalk, he headed up the street toward the gun shop, Rye Spurlock clinging to his arm like a troubled orphan. *We must look ridiculous,* he thought. But he, too, found himself darting sharp glances around him as he bought a box of eight-gauge wads from the gunsmith, then headed back down the street to the waiting coach. Rye stayed so close that she occasionally clipped his boot heels.

He was glad to finally help her aboard the stage. As she settled into her seat near the far window, facing the coach's rear, she seemed to sigh a little with relief.

Longarm tossed her carpetbag and leather grip into the boot.

"Got you a motherless duck there, Gus?" Johnny Anderson asked as Longarm stowed his own gear in the boot.

Longarm's glance caught on a dark shadow moving on the other side of the street, and his pulse quickened. But it was only a man in a long, green duster passing through a dense shade patch. No black-clad killer with a phony hand and a pronounced limp.

Flushing slightly, Longarm turned to the driver as Anderson tossed him an accordion bag from the small pile of luggage on the boardwalk fronting the station. McCallister frowned as he ran a pencil down his clipboard.

"I reckon," Longarm grunted, hefting the accordion bag into the boot.

The strongbox containing the gold bullion was already aboard, chained to the roof behind the driver's box. It had been secured there by the driver and shotgun rider who'd manned the trip's first leg from the mine at Talley to Rabbit Ridge. Both were now oiling their tonsils in the Prickly Pear Saloon, and no doubt waiting for the whores to wake up.

"I heard about the bloodbath in your room last night, Mr. Short," McCallister said with a knowing smirk as Longarm continued tossing luggage into the boot. "I hope you're not going to turn out to be a . . . troublemaker."

He gave another smirk, knowing full well that Longarm was a deputy U.S. marshal, but apparently wanting to play up the ruse for the others while giving the federal lawdog a little shit.

Longarm felt a spurt of irritation, but went along with the playacting by assuring his boss he didn't know who the would-be killers were but that he'd done nothing—nothing he knew about anyway—to provoke the attack.

"A godawful mess of blood," a woman's voice said. "I saw it this morning."

Longarm, McCallister, and Johnny Anderson all looked

at the lieutenant's wife, who was regarding Longarm with disapproval from the coach's rear window.

"Now, Danielle," the woman's husband said. "The man was only defending himself."

Longarm had learned his name was Lieutenant Dwight Fridley. He sat facing his wife from the opposite seat nearest the opposite front window, pomaded dark brown hair glistening in the morning sunshine.

"It was just a godawful amount of blood," Danielle said. "I'm from the city and completely unused to such frontier doings!"

Beyond her in the coach, the gambler and the two men dressed like drovers, and whose names Longarm hadn't learned yet, snickered. Rye Spurlock now sat in the coach's center, sort of hunkered down like she thought the sky was about to fall.

Mrs. Fridley glared at the gambler and two men with him and wrinkled her nose. "And you gentlemen might have bathed before boarding. I smell last night's alcohol on you, and the day hasn't even heated up yet!"

"Oh, boy," McCallister groaned, turning away. "Should be an interesting ride."

Anderson chuckled as he closed the coach door. Longarm glanced around as McCallister bade them a safe trip and began negotiating the tricky stairs rising to his second-story office.

No sign of Cormorant. No sign of more bushwhackers either.

"Any idea who they was, Gus?" Anderson asked when he and Longarm were both seated in the driver's boot above the snorting, tail-swishing horses. He must have noticed the pensive cast to Longarm's gaze as the lawman breeched the coach gun to check the loads for the third time that morning.

"Your guess is as good as mine," Longarm said.

"Didn't see you piss-burn anyone last night," said the driver, releasing the heavy brake with a grunt. "Less'n it happened before I was done crowin' upstairs."

"I was on relatively good behavior all day." Longarm jerked back in his seat as Anderson shook the reins over the six-hitch team's backs, and the stage rolled forward. He kicked the mail pouches under his seat. "Could just be the gun wolves decided to rid the stage of its shotgun guard before it even got moving."

"How'd they know we wouldn't get another one?"

"Good question," Longarm said. "I reckon we'll have to ask 'em when we see 'em."

Anderson laughed and shook his head. "I like you, Gus. You got a sense of humor!"

The team lurched into a lope. The barns and sheds and shabby frame houses of Rabbit Ridge pulled back behind the lumbering, clattering coach.

Longarm tipped his hat brim low and caressed the gut shredder's curved triggers, ignoring the hair prickling on the back of his neck.

They were off.

Chapter 10

Although the stage wouldn't enter the dangerous stretch of canyon fortuitously named Demon Rock until the third and final day of its journey, Longarm kept his eyes peeled on the terrain shifting around him.

There was nothing like the possibility of buying a bullet you wouldn't hear, and getting kicked out before you even knew what hit you, to keep every sense alive.

Every nerve curving toward the surface of the skin.

Every hair standing straight up beneath your collar.

Besides, there was a good possibility that the two men who'd ambushed him in the Prickly Pear had been sent by the stage-robbing trail wolves. The gang's method of operation so far had been to sharpshoot the shotgun rider in the canyon, but that didn't mean they hadn't decided to change tactics.

They might have figured that shooting the shotgun man the night before the stage was due to leave would give the company too little time to fill the man's boots. Especially since, so many shotgunners having been beefed before they could pick up their first paycheck, no one but a moron was likely to hire on.

That way, the gang could hit the virtually defenseless coach wherever it wanted.

The first day out of Rabbit Ridge, the trail wound over sage-stippled hogbacks and through canyons in the foothills of the Neversummer Mountains, with the fir-studded Snowy Range humping in the north. Occasionally, a small ranch appeared on the far horizon, and a prospector's shack could be seen at the bottom of a rocky ridge.

But mostly, what Longarm saw from his jostling perch in the driver's boot—sitting just right of Johnny Anderson, who handled the team like a seasoned jehu, armed with a blacksnake and bellowing curses at the tops of his lungs— were purple mountains rolling back behind occasional stony, shelving dikes and tabletop mesas.

There were plenty of vastly scattered cows and old buffalo trails. But as for men on horseback, Longarm spied only two. He took both to be cowboys walking their horses lazily over a distant butte shoulder, one twirling a rope over his head.

No sign of anyone dogging the coach's trail, and that included no black-clad gent with a bad leg and a wooden hand.

The stage stopped three times that first day, before stopping for the night at a motley station at the head of Beehive Gulch. They left early the next morning with a fresh team in the hitch. Now, as the coach climbed into rugged mountain country, the trail steepened and the horses grew weary.

Between relay station stops that second afternoon, Anderson drew rein at a shallow creek trickling over the trail, so the sweat-lathered pullers could have a badly needed drink and a ten-minute blow before continuing toward a razor-backed ridge. While Anderson adjusted the team's harnesses, the passengers left the stage to drink right along with the horses and to tend to nature.

The two cowboys and the gambler, who'd been drinking throughout the day so far, scattered into the brush. Longarm answered nature's call himself, and slipped behind a boulder not far from the trail.

He'd just gotten a good stream going, when footsteps sounded behind him. He jerked around, still pissing, to see Rye Spurlock standing a few feet away, looking customarily worried.

"You seen any sign of Cormorant?" she whispered, as though afraid the stalking half-breed himself might hear.

Longarm cursed and turned away to continue watering the sage in front of him. "Christ almighty—can a man have some privacy?"

"You ain't seen no sign of him, have ya, Gus?"

"No, I ain't seen no sign of him, Miss Rye, but if I do, you'll be the first to know."

"He's back there—I can smell him!"

Longarm glanced over his shoulder. "No doubt you can. Now, if you don't mind, you're startin' to inhibit my flow just a little."

"Gosh, I'm so sorry!"

Rye gave a caustic chuff and stomped off toward the stage on the other side of the rock. Longarm turned forward, and jerked back with a start. The lieutenant's wife, Danielle Fridley, stood not six feet in front of him. Her eyes were on his dribbling cock hanging out of his pants, and her cheeks were mottled red.

"Christ!" Longarm exclaimed.

She jerked her eyes up to his and manufactured a haughty look. "Rather an uncouth bastard, aren't you— evacuating your bladder out here where everyone can see?"

Longarm had started to tuck himself back into his pants, but stopped. He wasn't finished yet, and besides, he'd been here first.

He gave the woman a wolfish grin. "You're the one doin' the seein', Mrs. Fridley."

She turned, but not before giving his member one more glance, and stomped stiffly away. "Wait till your employer hears about this!"

Longarm chuckled and shook his head. Leave it to him to land the most bizarre assignment known to lawdogs past or present.

He shook the last dew from his lily, then walked a broad circle around the area to sniff out possible interlopers. Spying nothing but a couple of coyotes feeding on a dead fawn in a dry wash, and a diamondback sunning itself on a flat rock, he returned to the stage.

The passengers and Anderson had already climbed aboard, so he pulled himself up into the driver's box.

Anderson glanced at him, grinning shrewdly, as he field-stripped a quirley and let the breeze take the paper and tobacco. "Say, there, Gus. If'n you need me to take any o' them wimmen off your hands"—he tossed his head toward the coach roof—"you let me know."

With that, he grabbed up the reins and shook them over the team's backs, yelling, "Git up there, Nellie. Come on, Luke. *Mooove your lazy asses!*"

"I'd do that, Johnny," Longarm said as the coach splashed and rattled across the rocky stream. "But you're just too damn nice a guy."

The jehu tipped his hat low over his weathered, bearded face and laughed.

Near sunset that day, Johnny Anderson hoorawed the team around a long bend in the winding trail and into the yard of the overnight station identified as Hawk Ridge Station by a small wooden sign leaning along the trail's right side. There were a couple of bullet holes in the sign, but the place itself looked peaceful enough.

The cabin, barn, hay shed, and rail corrals sat in a well-sheltered canyon with steep granite walls on both sides. A creek sheathed in autumn yellow aspens ran to the left of the trail, while the station opened on the right, where the canyon bulged out away from the creek and where mostly sage and bunchgrass grew around the edges of the yard, which was hard-packed by many hooves and heavy, iron-shod stage wheels.

A good two dozen horses milled in two of the three corrals, and all twenty-four or so ran to the corral's near side, tails curled and ears pricked, several offering greeting whinnies, to which the stage's six-hitch team responded in kind.

The shrill but affable bugling echoed loudly off the canyon walls, for a moment drowning out the stream's steady, loud whisper in the aspens and the intermittent squawks of the windmill as a high breeze brushed its rooster tail.

An old, shaggy collie dog crawled stiffly out from beneath the two-story cabin's broad front porch, and trotted out to greet the coach and team, sending most of his half-hearted barks back over his shoulder toward the house. A big Indian in coveralls stepped outside the cabin, and a spindly little white woman followed, leaning on a cane and lifting a gnarled hand to shade her eyes from the sun just now dipping below the canyon's west wall.

Johnny Anderson hauled back on the reins to stop the team in the exact middle of the broad yard, near the clattering windmill. As the copper-tinted dust settled over him and Longarm, Johnny bellowed a greeting to the odd pair on the porch, then leaned toward Longarm, using the back of his gloved hand to muffle the words: "That's Tommy-John and Willa Ford. Willa's Tommy-John's mama. She married a Ute who's sick upstairs. Horse-kicked. Ain't spoke a word in two years."

He set the brake and wrapped the ribbons around the handle, turning to watch two bearded oldsters in shapeless hats wander out from the main barn—one tall and thin, one short and stocky and with a pinched-up face and near-white goat beard.

"Mind Miss Willa," Anderson told Longarm under his breath. "She's damn near a hundred years old, but she's a cranky old bat who's like to go after you with her shotgun if you so much cross your eyes at her. And she's got an eight-gauge to rival that one of yours, and I've seen her shoot it, too."

Longarm arched a curious brow at the jehu.

Anderson spoke again behind his gloved hand. "The old bat 'bout gave me a heart stroke, setting off both barrels of that damn thing when I was sittin' in her privy one mornin'. Sent double-aught buck screamin' over the roof. Said I was takin' too long, tyin' knots in her bowels, and 'no lady shits in a pail!'" He chuckled. "Holy God, I thought she was gonna reload and blow me to Kingdom Come!"

"Obliged for the warnin'," Longarm said, rising and doffing his hat to swipe the dust from his trousers.

Casting his glance around the yard, he froze suddenly.

A silhouetted figure was shuffling toward the main yard from the barn's shaded east wall. It was hard to tell for sure because of the poor light, but the man appeared to be dragging one foot. He also appeared to be wearing a hat that was only one shade lighter than the black of the barn shadows.

Longarm's heartbeat quickened. Half-standing, half-sitting, he dropped his hat and reached across his waist for the walnut-gripped .44 on his left hip. Anderson, who'd begun climbing out of the driver's box, stopped and frowned at Longarm.

As Longarm slipped the .44 from his holster, Anderson glanced over his shoulder. The black-clad gent stepped out into the wan sunlight—a tall, gangly kid in pin-striped coveralls and a gray linsey tunic. A small yellow dog had its jaws clamped down on the kid's coverall cuff, and the kid, giggling wildly through gritted teeth, dragged the snarling, growling pup out into the yard.

"Oh, that's just Pip," Anderson said, jerking his thumb over his shoulder. "He's a moron kid some rancher around here kicked out of his cabin. Willa took him in to muck out the barn and wash dishes an' such. Ain't good for much else."

Longarm slid his Colt back into its holster as the tall Pip walked up, still dragging the playful little cur, to help the two old hostlers unhitch the team. Longarm's cheeks warmed with chagrin. He'd never known himself to be so jumpy.

Grunting a curse, he climbed down the coach's right side, planted a boot on the wheel, then leaped the last two feet to the ground. Rye Spurlock and her overactive imagination had him slapping iron on cork-headed younkers now.

As Longarm opened the coach door so the passengers could step down, the spidery old woman came clomping down the porch steps, stooped over like a hunchback, her washed-out blue eyes boring holes into the jehu, who'd gone to the coach's rear to unload the luggage boot.

"Johnny Anderson, you're damn near forty-five minutes late. Me and Tommy-John was beginning to think you'd been run down by them brigands prowlin' the trail."

"Now, Miss Willa," Anderson said, dropping a couple of carpetbags to the ground. "You know how rough this trail can be. We run across a coupla washouts—must have had a pretty good rain in these parts in the last few days—and we had to ease down a bit. Wouldn't want us to crack a wheel or an axle now, would ya? Or bring one o' the hosses up lame?"

"You always got somethin' to say in defense of your feeble ass, don't ya, Johnny?"

Anderson glanced at Longarm, who was helping Mrs. Fridley out of the stage, the woman's eyes icy and disapproving. Anderson winked as he continued removing the luggage from the boot while addressing Miss Willa.

"Speakin' o' them owlhoots, ma'am—you ain't seen no suspicious characters around of late, have you?"

"You know me, Johnny—if I see any suspicious characters, I put my Greener to 'em. I don't put up with no suspicious nonsense at my station. I say when in doubt shoot first and ask no questions, and have Tommy-John dig a real deep hole."

The old woman threw her withered head as far back on her humped shoulders as it would go, and cackled like a scalded chicken. When her choked guffaws had died, she glanced at Rye Spurlock and Danielle Fridley, giving both women the quick, cold up-and-down. They were standing near the stage, Lieutenant Fridley between them, looking around skeptically at the run-down cabin, the stone chimney gushing thick gray smoke.

"You men are responsible for your own women," Miss Willa warned Longarm and the others. "My boys get ganders at skirts and corsets right seldom—'ceptin' mine, that is—so you just watch these two little prissy-pusses your ownselves. Don't let 'em outta your sight. I take no responsibility for their welfare!"

Unhitching the team, the two old hostlers chuckled. Pip, glassy-eyed, regarded the women while chewing his lower lip. The yellow pup sat in the dirt beside him, its eyes, too, on the two women, tipping its head with its dirty snout this way and that. The big half-breed son of Miss Willa just stood atop the cabin's front porch, stone-faced.

"Come along now—I don't serve supper all goddamn evenin'!"

With that, Miss Willa turned and stomped back to the cabin.

Longarm glanced at Johnny Anderson, who laughed. "Ain't she prime?"

Chapter 11

In the side shed off Hawk Ridge Station's main barn, Long-arm snapped his eyes open.

He was sleeping out here to be close to—and alone with—the bullion-bearing strongbox that he and Anderson had stowed under the side shed room's lone cot. There being no safe on the premises, they figured the gold would be safer here than in the house, where any would-be night-attacking thieves would look for it first.

Longarm lifted his head from the cot's musty pillow and reached for the double-barreled coach gun. He'd heard something in the main barn—a faint rasping sound, like that of a slowly opening door. Dropping his bare feet to the floor, he looked around the unfamiliar room to get his bearings. Milky moonlight angled through the room's single window, directly across the room from the cot. He could see the narrow door to his right, in the same wall the cot abutted, about eight feet away.

There was a sharp click as someone tripped the door's leather and steel latch.

Longarm bounded to his feet and tiptoed over behind the

door as its hinges began to groan. In the moonlight, he watched the plank door move slowly toward him. Straw and grit crunched as the person behind the door stole into the room. Longarm aimed the gut shredder's double barrels on the silhouetted figure, earing both hammers back.

They clicked loudly in the room's dense silence.

Longarm said, "Stop right there less'n you want me to open a hole in your back big enough to run a train through."

He'd no sooner said it before the moonlight fell over thick blond hair and, swinging toward him, Rye Spurlock said, "Don't shoot, Gus—it's me, Rye!"

Longarm shouldered the door closed and lowered the shotgun. "Goddamn it, Miss Rye—you're gonna be the death of me yet," he complained. "I told you to stay inside. What the hell you doin' out here anyways?"

"That big half-breed, Tommy-John, was givin' me the eye all night. I was just sittin' downstairs in front of the fire, mindin' my own business and darnin' a sock while the other men played cards, and he wouldn't take his eyes off my titties. I'm afraid of him, Gus, and I can't sleep!"

"Hell, Johnny'll protect you from Tommy-John."

"Ha! Him and them two old codgers are up there sawin' wood so loud they're like to wake the dead! I don't know how Mrs. Fridley and Miss Willa can stand it!"

"Ah, shit. I suppose you're wantin' to sleep out here."

Rye stepped toward him and began fiddling with the open buttons on the V neck of his wash-worn longhandles. "Would you mind?"

Longarm cursed under his breath. It was going to be damn hard to get any sleep with Rye out here in all her comely, sexy beauty. And to be wide awake on the trail tomorrow necessitated a good night's rest. But he knew when he was beaten.

"All right, all right." Longarm gestured at the cot. "Help yourself."

"Thanks, Gus."

"Don't mention it."

When Rye had undressed down to her underwear and slipped under the cot's two wool blankets, Longarm looked at her for a moment. She lay there on the far side of the narrow cot, her curvaceous figure delineated by the moonlight, resting her head on the heel of her hand as she stared expectantly up at him. Her rich, blond hair tumbled over her hand and forearm, and fanned across the far end of Longarm's pillow.

Her camisole billowed out from her chest, and he could see way down into her cleavage. He could also see her nipples like buttons through the light cotton fabric.

"Christ." With effort, Longarm turned away from the girl and stepped into his trousers.

"What are you doing?" Rye asked.

"Gonna go out and get some air, have a look around. Smoke a cigar." Longarm sat in a creaky Windsor chair to pull his socks on. "You get yourself some sleep."

"Oh, but, Gus, I was sorta hopin' we could . . ."

"I got a job to do, and you, Miss Rye, are not makin' it easy."

"I don't mean to be a distraction, Gus."

"I'm sure you don't, Miss Rye. Just the same, you go on and go to sleep while I step out for a little air."

With that, he stomped into his boots, grabbed the big coach gun and his hat, and opened the door. The girl gave a heated chuff behind him as he closed the plank-board door and began tramping through the barn's dense darkness, relieved here and there by moonlight angling through a sashed window, toward the front.

He slipped out the big front doors and stood just in front of them, taking a deep draught of the cool, fresh night air that smelled of rotting leaves and the nearby stream. The three-quarter moon was so bright, it blotted out most of the stars. It shone eerily bright on the station yard, pushing out deep, velvet shadows from the corrals and outbuildings. It washed over the roof of the cabin on the other side of the yard like a liquid pearl.

A faint breeze rustled the tops of the cottonwoods—a very light, scratching, rustling sound. From far off, Longarm could hear two dogs barking—one deep and throaty, the other higher-pitched. Probably the old dog and the pup from the station out treeing coons along the creek farther up the canyon.

Longarm turned to see a couple of the corraled horses hanging their heads over the top rail, staring toward him. They looked calm enough. He could even see a couple sprawled on their sides, asleep.

If something were amiss out here—if the trail wolves or a lone, limping gunman were stalking the station—the horses would be the first to indicate it.

"At ease, fellas," Longarm told the horses twitching their ears at him curiously. "Just fleein' the beautiful girl in my bed."

He chuckled dryly and walked out away from the barn, looking around the yard's western edge before stopping and opening his fly buttons to relieve himself. When he finished, he walked a little farther along the trail, looking around and listening, then sat on a boulder beside the trail under a giant cottonwood. He dug a half-smoked cheroot out of his shirt pocket, scraped a match to life on his thumbnail, and drew a deep lungful of the peppery smoke.

He'd taken a couple more heady drags before a door latch clicked loudly in the deep, dark silence.

He glanced toward the cabin to see the front door swing inward. Wan lamplight shone in the opening before it was blocked by a slender finger. The person sort of stumbled out the door, drew it hastily closed, and descended the porch steps quickly, almost tripping, hard-soled shoes clattering on the half-rotted wood.

When the person stepped out from under the shading porch roof and into the moonlit yard, Longarm saw long, dark brown hair tumbling to narrow shoulders.

Mrs. Fridley.

She wore the wool traveling dress she'd been wearing earlier, and she held a blanket around her shoulders. She stopped at the bottom of the porch steps and lowered her head suddenly. The breeze picked up just then, so it was hard for Longarm to tell for sure, but he thought he heard the woman loose a shrill sob. It was like the chirp of a small bird.

Then, Danielle Fridley stumbled forward and, holding the blanket tightly about her shoulders, strode across the yard, head bowed, and stopped before the corral off the barn's far side. In the moonlight, Longarm saw her head bob and her shoulders jerk.

Longarm drew another slow drag from the nickel cheroot, watching the woman with his eyes narrowed in speculation. Now, what the hell was Mrs. Fridley so distraught about that she'd venture into a remote stage station yard at midnight?

Longarm sat the boulder and rolled the cigar in his teeth for a time. Then, his curiosity getting the better of him, he rubbed the coal out on the boulder, returned the cheroot to his shirt pocket, hung the double-bore gut shredder by its bandolier lanyard over his shoulder, and rose to mosey in the woman's direction.

He was within a few yards of Danielle Fridley, who now leaned forward against the corral, audibly sobbing and sniffling, when she lifted her head suddenly and shot a frightened glance over her shoulder.

Longarm stopped. "Just me, ma'am—Gus Short."

"Oh," she said with a sniff. Her eyes dropped to his boots, then rose to his face. "It's you. Don't you sleep, Mr. Short?" She turned to him suddenly, splaying her fingers across her breasts. "Oh, heavens—you haven't seen—?"

"No, ma'am. No sign of trouble. I was just . . . uh . . . gettin' some air. Couldn't help seein' you leave the cabin. You appeared sort of . . . well . . . sort of troubled."

She sobbed and turned away suddenly, prodding her front teeth with the tip of her thumb. A flame-shaped boulder and a cottonwood stood just off the corner of the corral, and she staggered off into the shadows there and leaned against the corral's corner post. Her shoulders jerked as she held a hand to her mouth, not tightly enough to completely muffle her continued sobbing.

Longarm sighed as he adjusted the weight of the shotgun on his shoulder. Whatever had the woman so distraught wasn't his business. She'd probably argued with her husband. Or maybe she was just one of those overly emotional females for whom a change in the weather caused inexplicable panic.

"Ma'am, I do sympathize with your anguish, but I suggest you go back inside. I'm gonna head back to bed my ownself and . . ."

He let the sentence trail off as the woman's sobs grew louder.

Longarm sighed, glanced at the barn, then turned back

to the woman. Cursing under his breath, he stepped forward. Concealed by the cottonwood's shadows, Danielle Fridley leaned her forehead against the corral's top rail, sniffling.

Longarm tapped her shoulder. "Look, Mrs.—"

She turned to him suddenly, teeth gritted. She let the blanket drop from her shoulders. She wore only a very thin chemise above her skirt, revealing her fine, long neck, broad shoulders, and a good portion of freckled cleavage. She grabbed Longarm's shirt in her fists and pulled him against her.

"Fuck me, damn you. If my husband won't do it, surely I can coerce the shotgun man." She jerked the shocked, incredulous Longarm toward her, glaring up at him. "Fuck me, damn you. I need a real man's rod between my legs!"

Her voice broke on this last, and she reached up and wrapped her arms around Longarm's neck, pulling his head down and clamping her mouth over his. She shoved her tongue into his mouth, grabbed his left hand, and clamped it over her breast.

Longarm kept his hand there on her breast even after she released it. He was a man, after all. And he couldn't help returning the woman's savage kiss either, feeling his dong stiffening.

Kissing him hungrily, she clamped both her hands on his ass and kneaded his buttocks through his pants before snaking her hands around his hips and digging at his fly buttons. "Give it to me, damnit," she ordered through gritted teeth. "I need some satisfaction, for chrissakes, and I know you can satisfy me with *this*!"

As she said "this," she reached into his pants and wrapped her cool hand around his cock. She gave a shudder and pulled out the appendage she'd been searching for, pumping it hungrily. Longarm drew a sharp breath. He felt his shaft grow harder in spite of the woman's cold hand and the brusqueness with which she manipulated him.

The ole trouser snake truly did have a mind of its own, for the rest of him knew he should walk—no, *run!*—away from the woman—another *crazy* one, for sure!—and hide himself till morning in the barn. But the rest of him was at the mercy of his cock, so when she started to unbutton her skirt and then drop it before going to work on her pantaloons, he did nothing to stop her. In fact, he found himself kneading her warm, swollen breasts through her cotton camisole.

A few seconds later, after her pantaloons had joined her skirt on the ground, he hoisted her up onto his cock, then turned and shoved her back up against the trunk of the cottonwood tree.

"Oh, you fucker," Danielle Fridley cried, wrapping her bare legs around his waist, her arms around his neck, as he began to bounce her up and down. "Oh, Mother of Christ, you're a fucker! Oh, fuck me, fuck me—*harder, harder, harder!*"

As Longarm strong-armed the woman up and down on his cock, her hair tumbled around her shoulders and over her face. Her naked breasts bounced, nipples jutting. She gritted her teeth and threw her head back on her shoulders, wailing loudly enough that Longarm was afraid she'd wake the cabin.

He pressed her harder against the tree and pulled her abruptly against him, thrusting his hips forward and burying himself deep inside her. She squealed and dug her heels even harder into his back as he fired off inside her, and she quivered against him like a very large fish at the end of a line.

When they'd both finished, exhausted, she opened her eyes. They focused somewhere behind him. "Okay, Wilbur," she sighed.

Bewildered, Longarm glanced over his shoulder.

He only glimpsed the brass-plated rifle butt darting toward his forehead before everything went black and quiet.

Chapter 12

A raucous cawing shriek echoed off the tender inside walls of Longarm's head, flaming the fire behind his eyes.

He jerked his chin off the ground with a start and felt something sharp digging into his shoulder. He caught a sidelong glimpse of the flat, round face of a snowy owl. He smelled the musty fetor. Automatically, he jerked his arm up.

"I ain't dead yet, you carrion-eatin' son of a bitch!"

Another raking yowl assaulted him, penetrating the core of his very being, as a wing smashed against his face with one windy beat, and then the two spidery, clawed feet kicked off his shoulder, feeling as though they were ripping out a goodly clump of skin and muscle as they did.

There was yet another ear-raking shriek that echoed around the station yard and made Longarm grit his teeth against the aggravated throbbing in his head. And then the bird was gone—a large, pale gray shadow swooping up over the corral and the standing horses and the barn's eerily moonlit roof.

The nocturnal raptor sent one last cry reverberating from

up the canyon. The sound dwindled quickly as the bird winged northward.

Longarm groaned and rolled onto his back. He brought a hand to his throbbing forehead, felt the goose egg just below his hairline. It ached like an exposed tooth nerve probed by a sadistic dentist, and he jerked his hand away from it.

"What in the name of . . . ?"

Then he remembered the rifle's brass butt plate jabbing toward his head. He remembered then, too, what he'd been doing just before that unceremonious meeting of his head and the rifle butt, and chagrin swept over him like a porcupine robe with all the quills attached.

"Good Christ," he croaked, pushing himself up onto his knees and looking around. "What in the hell did I go and do now?"

The moon had angled a good distance over the barn. He must have been out an hour or more. Wincing, blinking against the hammering in his swollen forehead, he heaved himself up to his feet and looked around once more as though he might still catch a glimpse of Danielle Fridley and whoever had rammed the rifle butt against his head.

Of course, he saw nothing but the corral and the horses—most of whom stared at him with dull curiosity—and the big cottonwood and the boulder off the corral's corner post. And the moonlit and shadow-laden yard.

The cabin was dark and quiet. So, too, was the barn.

The barn.

The bullion under his cot in the barn . . .

Ah, Christ, Longarm, you stupid, randy son of a bitch. What'd you go and do now?

He remembered the big coach gun, and after a quick

look around, found it lying in the shadow of the boulder where it had apparently fallen. Vaguely wondering why whoever had hit him hadn't taken it, he picked it up, brushed it off, and began tramping dazedly, cursing himself under his breath, toward the barn.

He had to slow his pace or take broad steps to each side when the ground pitched around him, to keep from falling. When he made the barn, he nearly collapsed against the two large closed doors. When he got one open, he stepped inside and stumbled back toward the side shed, the moonlight still angling through the windows keeping him from ramming stall partitions and ceiling joists.

Holding his breath in dread, he shoved open the side-shed door.

There was a muffled cry, and Longarm turned to see a blond-headed figure humped on the cot. Moving closer, he saw that Rye Spurlock had been hogtied and gagged. She jerked around on her side, shaking her head desperately and grunting loudly behind the neckerchief someone had tied over her mouth and around her head.

Longarm set the shotgun against the wall, grabbed his barlow knife from his coat pocket, opened it, and quickly sawed through the rope binding the girl's hands and feet. When he'd freed her limbs, he flipped the gag up over her head.

"Gus!" the girl cried, throwing herself against Longarm's chest and wrapping her arms around him tightly. She convulsed, sobbing. "I thought those bastards were gonna kill me!"

"What bastards, Miss Rye?"

Her breasts heaved against his chest. He could feel her tears through his shirt. Longarm grabbed her shoulders and held her away from him, crouching to stare into her face. He shook her gently, and her hair flopped around her tear-streaked cheeks.

"Miss Rye, what bastards? Who where they? How many?"

"It was that Lieutenant Fridley. Him and three other gents I never seen before. Them and Fridley's wife. They come in here and held guns on me—the woman, she held a big old pistol right in my face and told me if I made a sound she'd blow a third eye in my head. One I couldn't *see* through!"

As the girl convulsed again and clutched at Longarm's shirt, the lawman shook her gently once more to get her attention. "Okay, Miss Rye. I'm sure it was right terrifying. But I really need to know—"

"They took the box out from under the cot!"

Longarm's heart turned a somersault in his chest. He winced, biting his lower lip. "Yeah, I had a feelin' they didn't come in here just to toss you around a little."

He released the girl, lifted the drooping blankets up over the cot, and peered beneath. Just like he'd figured—and just like Rye had said—the strongbox was gone.

Longarm looked at the girl, who sat with her pantaloon-clad legs curled on the cot, breathing hard, pulling her hair back from her face, and trying to compose herself. "Three other gents besides the lieutenant and Mrs. Fridley, eh?" Longarm asked her.

"Yep." Rye nodded and sniffed. "The woman wanted to kill me, but the lieutenant wouldn't let her do it. The ring-tailed polecat said they should've killed you, too, but one of the other men—they was all dressed in dark suits—said they wasn't in this to hang, and they'd be a long ways away from here by the time you had your wits back. It wasn't your job to track 'em anyways, they said."

She shook her head and clawed again at Longarm's shirt. "What'd they do to you, Gus? What kind of horrible things did they do to you out there?"

Longarm's ears burned as he gained his feet and turned to the window. "Oh, I'll get over it," he growled, peering out into the side yard, at the cottonwoods silhouetted against the moonlit sky.

Quickly, he thought through his options.

He grabbed his gunbelt off a coat peg and wrapped it around his waist. "Miss Rye, I want you to go back into the house, but I don't see much point in waking the others. What I gotta do, I gotta do alone. Let 'em wake up on their own come mornin'."

He buckled the cartridge belt, then produced his leather wallet from an inside coat pocket. Dropping to one knee in front of the cot, he opened the wallet and held his badge up in front of Rye's moist, bright-eyed face.

"You see that, Miss Rye? That's my badge. I'm not Gus Short, like I been leadin' you and the others to believe. My name is Custis Long. I'm a deputy United States marshal. Up to now, I've kept my true identity secret so there'd be no way for the trail wolves to know a lawman was riding the stage in the guise of a shotgun guard. Might've affected their way of going about things, don't ya know. Anyway, what I want you to do is very important, so listen very carefully, all right?"

Rye frowned at the badge pinned to the inside of Longarm's wallet and nodded her head slowly.

"Come morning, I want you to tell Johnny Anderson what happened out here tonight. Then I want you to tell

him I'm a lawman and that I went after the five owlhoots
who stole the strongbox. Tell him to sit tight. I don't care
about his timetable. Tell him to sit tight right here at the
station until I get back with the bullion. Can you do that for
me, Miss Rye?"

"You're . . . Custis P. Long . . . ?"

"That's right."

"A U.S. *lawman*?"

Longarm sighed in frustration. "That's right. Now, did
you hear what else I just said?"

"Jesus," Rye said wonderingly, "I *screwed* a United
States *lawman*?"

Longarm's ears started burning anew, kicking up the
horrible throbbing in his swollen forehead. "I was undercover at the time, Miss Rye, and I was afraid that if I re-
fused you I might blow my cover. Anyway, that doesn't
matter just now. Did you hear what I told you?"

She sniffed and shook her hair away from her face.
"Wait till mornin' and then tell the driver to sit tight and wait
for you."

"You got it." Longarm grabbed the coach gun and
started shoving shotgun wads into his coat pockets. He'd
have to saddle a horse in a hurry and start tracking. He
didn't want the Fridleys and the other three owlhoots to get
too far away.

Thank God there was a good moon at least.

"Gus—" The girl stopped, shook her head. "I mean,
Marshal Long . . ."

Longarm stopped at the door. "Call me Longarm. Everyone else does."

"Longarm, I'm really frightened," Rye whined. "I mean,
you're goin' off after them polecats, leavin' me here in the
dark night, and right this very minute Weed Cormorant

could be out creepin' around, lookin' for me to hogtie me and take me away to his lair!"

Longarm wrung the shotgun in his hands. "He ain't out there, Miss Rye. I been out there quite a while and I ain't seen hide nor hair of him. Besides, you'll be safe in the cabin."

"Will you escort me inside?"

Longarm swallowed down his impatience. "All right, but let's make it quick!"

When he had Rye Spurlock safely inside the cabin, from which he could hear the men's snores emanating as far out as the windmill, he chose what looked to be a good, stout-legged, broad-barreled saddle horse, and quickly leathered it. On foot, he cut the sign of six shod horses, which meant the gang had probably brought an extra horse for hauling the heavy strongbox.

The three well-dressed outlaws must have been waiting out by the creek on the far side of the canyon. They'd likely pulled all six horses up to the yard when one of them, probably Lieutenant Fridley—if that's who he really was—had brained Longarm just after he'd finished fucking the lieutenant's wife.

If she'd really been the man's wife, which wasn't probable. If she had been, Longarm would likely be food right now for that hungry barn owl.

Mounting the steeldust he'd chosen for his wild ride, Longarm followed the six sets of tracks by moonlight out into the cottonwoods and then swung westward, following the tracks westward out of the canyon. As he rode, he tried to get his mind off his throbbing noggin and the feeling of profound foolishness at getting himself hornswoggled like he had. The woman had likely seen him in the yard, then come out and feigned sadness to draw him toward her.

He wondered if the lieutenant and Mrs. Fridley were part of the same gang of trail wolves that had been haunting the stage line of late, or part of some other group invading the first group's territory.

The latter seemed more likely. The strategy here was just too different from that of the veteran bullion thieves.

He could tell by the widely spread hoofprints that the six horses had lit a fast shuck out of the stage station, using the moonlight to their best advantage. Longarm rode just as fast, propelled by fury, though he had to slow often to make sure he was still on the trail.

He stopped once to drink and bathe his burning forehead at a spring, and to toss back a couple of pain-relieving shots from the bottle of Maryland rye he kept wrapped in heavy burlap in his saddlebags. Then he pushed on, through a couple of canyons and across a narrow, moonlit valley, riding what he judged was a good fifteen miles from the station.

Eight thirty the next morning found him cresting a steep hill somewhere north and west of his starting point, in a jog of low, pine-studded ridges and shrub-choked canyons.

Pushing on over the ridge and several yards down the other side, so the sky wouldn't outline him, he halted the weary steeldust in a thick snag of chokecherries and pitted granite boulders. He stared over one such boulder, into the V-shaped wedge of canyon below, where a stream meandered over rocks, glistening with morning sunshine. A few aspens stood along the stream, lazily shedding their glowing yellow leaves.

Around a bend in the stream and over a sloping shoulder of the far ridge, smoke rose. It climbed just over the shoulder from the other side—a thick swirl of white smoke that danced in the breeze before dispersing against the cobalt sky.

Longarm's heart quickened. It aggravated the ache in his head. Fortunately, however, it was only an ache, the throbbing having abated overnight, doubtless helped along by several more pulls from his rye bottle.

What hadn't been quelled, however, was his blistering fury at Danielle Fridley, or whoever she was, for having led him into such an embarrassing trap.

He was just damn glad there hadn't been anyone else around to see him take that post-coital braining.

He stepped down from the saddle and tied the steeldust to a shrub, well concealed from below, and considered whether he should take the coach gun that he'd been carrying all night, or the Winchester '73 snugged down in his saddle boot.

The rifle would work best at long range. But he chose the coach gun.

He intended to get close.

Real close.

And if any of the five who'd made a fool out of him didn't like it, he . . . or she . . . would go the way of the two bushwhacking owlhoots back in Longarm's hotel room in Rabbit Ridge—turned to human sieves by eight-gauge buck!

Chapter 13

A knee-numbing, brain-addling hiss sounded—raspy and dark with portent.

Crawling down the slope toward the outlaws' fire, Longarm stopped in his tracks, the big shotgun held crosswise before him, lanyard around his neck. He turned his gaze to the right, and miniature javelins of black fire spurted through his veins when he saw the rattler coiled atop a ground-level rock about ten feet away.

The snake lifted its striated tail and shifted its flat head this way and that, its penny-colored, pellet-sized eyes riveted on the lawman. Gently, Longarm drew the shotgun back toward him and swung the barrel toward the viper.

He was close enough to the outlaws that he could hear them caterwauling around their cookfire, and their horses stomping, blowing, and slurping water from a spring. Obviously, the coach gun's blast would alert them to his presence.

So he had a choice—either let himself get bit by this damn viper, his second in nearly as many days, or shoot the snake and get beefed by the outlaws in the company of the diabolical Mrs. Fridley.

His partly swollen cheek still aching where the last snake had dry-bit him, Longarm halfheartedly aimed the shotgun at the rattling serpent before him, keeping the big blaster close to his chest so as not to threaten the viper further.

"Ouch!" one of the men howled at the bottom of the slope. "Damnit, Danielle, that hurt. You durn near put my eye out!"

A woman laughed. Then Danielle Fridley's voice exclaimed, "With the money you got now, Wilbur, you can buy you a brand-new glass one that's a whole lot prettier'n your own!"

Another man added to the conversation, but Longarm stopped listening. For the moment, he was more interested in the snake than the outlaws. The last thing he needed was an arm or a cheek pumped full of diamondback-brand tanglefoot. He doubted he'd get as lucky as the last time he'd encountered such a scaly, rock-colored demon.

If he had to, he'd blast the viper to a fine red spray, then rely on the gut shredder's remaining barrel and his Frontier Colt to do battle with the outlaws. Likely, he couldn't get all five without the element of surprise, but he wasn't about to let this viper sink its teeth in, assuring him a very slow and painful, howling death out here in the middle of nowhere.

Only vaguely did he ruminate on the troublesome nature of his current assignment. Lately, his missions had been getting so treacherous that he'd begun to wonder if someone in the Federal Building wasn't trying to get him greased—his boss, Billy Vail, or Billy's typewriter-banging secretary, Henry.

Or had Denver's founding father, General William Larimer, finally found out that Longarm had been routinely fucking his favorite niece doggie-style behind the general's back, and been pushing buttons and turning levers in the First District Court of Colorado to land Longarm the deadliest assignments known to badge-sporting lawdogs?

The snake stopped shaking its tail suddenly. Then, just as suddenly, and just as Longarm had begun to slowly ear back the barn blaster's left hammer, the snake lowered its head and slithered away through the clumps of sage and rabbit brush. Longarm stared after the deadly critter, his lower jaw hanging.

He chuffed with relief, felt every drawn-taut muscle in his frame slowly uncoil. That was a bit of unusual good luck. Well, back to business. Rising up on his elbows, he resumed slithering snakelike himself down the hill, meandering around rocks and shrubs and keeping both eyes peeled for more deadly man-traps.

A few minutes later, at the bottom of the canyon, he crawled up between two large wolf willow shrubs. Doffing his hat and keeping his head low, he stared into the willow-sheathed clearing before him in which the outlaws' coffee fire snapped and popped, and a black coffeepot chugged and hissed.

The six horses were hobbled on the far side of the fire, beyond more shrubs. Around the fire, Danielle Fridley sat, dressed in a long wool skirt and buckskin shirt, with a man's felt Stetson on her pretty head. Her hair hung loose about her shoulders. She sat on a rock, just now tipping a whiskey bottle over her steaming coffee cup.

Her husband, if that's who he really was, knelt beside the fire, stirring a pot of bubbling beans with a long stick. Fridley no longer wore his lieutenant's uniform, but black denims with a black buscadero rig on his narrow hips. He wore a pinstriped shirt, brown vest, and a black, funnel-brimmed hat from which the feather of a red-tailed hawk protruded.

The other three gents were all dressed, as Rye had indicated, in three-piece suits. They looked like bad gamblers. One wore orange-and-black-checked pants and a clawhammer coat. He had a patch over one eye, a long spade beard, and a sweeping mustache. He sat on a rock far left of the fire, running a rag over the big horse pistol in his hands.

One of the other suit-clad gents slept nearby, snoring softly, head against his saddle, brown hat pulled low over his sunburned face. The third man was standing off to the right, pissing on a sage shrub. He was short and stocky, and a sawed-off, double-barreled shotgun dangled from a leather lanyard down his back. His green-checked suit coat, grimy with dirt and sweat, matched his trousers, the cuffs of which were stuffed down into his knee-high, lace-up boots.

As Danielle set the bottle at her feet, she glanced at the chained and padlocked strongbox beside her. "What do you fellas say we blow the lock off the box here, divide the takin's, and split up? Just in case someone's foggin' our backtrail?"

Her careful, cultivated speech and tone had evaporated. She now spoke with as much salt and vinegar as Rye Spurlock, and Longarm detected more than a little Texas accent.

"Ah, shit—who'd be after us way out here?" asked the pissing outlaw, glancing over his shoulder. A half-smoked, loosely rolled quirley drooped from his mouth.

"The shotgun guard—that's who," Danielle barked, tossing her head toward Fridley kneeling beside the fire. "If Cousin Wilbur here had let me kill the son of a bitch, we wouldn't have anything to worry about. But he's the type that's gonna take it personal—bein' fucked and knocked senseless like that, his strongbox bein' stole out from under him. Mark my words. I can tell by the way he threw the blocks to me!"

"Thought you enjoyed it," Wilbur said with a chuckle.

"I did enjoy it. Almost as much as you enjoyed watchin', you little pervert. First real man I had since Tascosa. But you shoulda let me kill him, Wilbur, you weak-livered son of a bitch!"

Wilbur bolted to his feet, his face pinched and red with anger. "You quit callin' me names, Danielle. Goddamnit, I won't stand for it. I ain't gonna hang for killin' some no-'count shotgun rider. You can fuck 'em all you want, but I ain't gonna let you kill 'em no more. I'll lie, cheat, and steal same as always, but I'm done killin'. It keeps me awake at night—thinking about that gray-bearded executioner tying the noose around my neck and dropping the floor out from under my boots!"

He was nearly crying at that last, so Longarm saw his opening.

"*U.S. marshal!*" he bellowed, shoving his cheek up taut to the shotgun's stock and aiming down the broad double barrels. "Nobody move or I'll blow train tunnels through your briskets!"

"What the fuck?" Danielle screeched, dropping her coffee cup and bolting to her feet.

At the same time, the suited gent cleaning his pistol also bolted to his feet, looking around until his narrowed, dung brown eyes picked Longarm out of the foliage. "*Son of a bitch!*" he screamed.

As the suited gent began to extend the big horse pistol in his right hand, Longarm tripped the shotgun's left trigger.

KABOOM!

The suited gent was thrown straight back as though he'd been mown down by an invisible locomotive tearing through the clearing at sixty miles per hour. A wink later, the man who'd been draining the dragon dropped to a crouch, squaring his shoulders at Longarm and reaching for the holstered .44 tucked down over his belly.

KABOOM!

He, too, was hammered back through the willows and out of sight, setting the horses to screaming.

"No!" Wilbur Fridley screamed, staggering backward and holding his arms in front of his face.

Danielle Fridley just stood there, hands hanging down over the two holsters thonged low on her slender thighs. Her face was ghostly white, and her lips were pinched like a schoolmarm's.

Longarm didn't have time to examine either her or her cousin Wilbur closely, as the third gent, the one who'd been sawing logs to the left of the fire, had sat up quickly, eyes blazing as he reached for the Buntline Special resting on a rock beside him.

"Uh-uh!" Longarm warned, dropping the coach gun and climbing quickly to his knees, grinding his teeth at the misery the twin blasts of the gut shredder had set up in his head. He filled his right fist with his Frontier Colt .44, but not before the suited gent snapped off an echoing blast with his long-barreled bowel-tickler.

The bullet caromed over Longarm's left shoulder to *ping* off a rock behind him.

The lawman winced, crouched, and fanned off three quick shots. All three slugs tore through the suited gent's torso and laid him out against his saddle, as though he'd suddenly decided to ignore the hubbub and return to his slumber.

The nap didn't last long, however. He groaned, clutching one of the wounds low in his chest, and flopped over onto his belly. He began crawling back toward the willows and the horses, moving one long leg at a time, like a turtle heading for water.

"You killed me, you son of a bitch!" he sobbed.

Longarm slid his smoking .44 toward Danielle, who had closed one hand over one of her low-slung Schofields. "Go ahead," he growled, narrowing one eye against the pick that a miniature prospector was assaulting the backside of his forehead with. "I'd really like you to do that, Danielle. Go ahead and pull that hogleg, and let me plant a pill between your purty tits."

"Don't shoot, mister," Wilbur said, holding his hands high in the air and cutting his eyes nervously between Longarm and Danielle. "I'm done. I'm through. My nerves are done shot, and I don't want no more o' this bullshit. I can't take it anymore."

Danielle removed her hand from her gun and glanced at her cousin, sneering. "Shut the fuck up, you damn fool. It is over—can't you see?" She turned to Longarm, who was stepping out of the bushes, holding his .44 out from his right hip. "Unless Gus here wants another fuck? How 'bout it, Gus? I'll fuck you again if you promise to turn me loose."

"Nah," Longarm said. "I been fucked over pretty good already. But if you don't unbuckle those gunbelts—both o' you cousins—I'll drill you right here and make my job a whole lot more simple."

"Son of a bitch killed me!" This from the wounded

suited gent who'd crawled as far as the willows and stopped. He'd turned onto one side, writhing and crossing his arms on his chest as if to hold the blood in. "He done killed me. Can't y'all see how I'm dyin' here?"

"We see, Waco," Danielle said, unbuckling her cartridge belt. "And we wish you'd get it over with and shut the fuck up."

Her guns and belt dropped in the dirt with a plop and dust puff. Wilbur's followed.

They both stood there—Danielle behind the fire, Wilbur to the left side of it—holding their hands up. Wilbur held his higher than his cousin's, looking grim and frightened. For her part, Danielle only sneered at Longarm, her eyes cool and mocking.

"Well, if another fuck don't entice ya," she said as Longarm moved slowly forward, "how 'bout we split the bullion? No lawman I've ever known—and I should've known you was one, since you got the look an' all—ever made near as much money as you'd make from a three-way split of what's in the strongbox there. Shit, we all three could go down to Mexico and live like royals."

She grinned mischievously and cocked one boot. "And, who knows, you might forgive me for pussy-whippin' you earlier and come to like my pussy again right fine."

Chapter 14

Longarm chuckled at the girl's invitation.

He had to admit she was a saucy thing—nearly as sexy as Rye Spurlock, but without Rye's tender, vulnerable innocence. But even if Danielle had been more like Rye, he wouldn't have given her proposition even halfhearted consideration. He was many things at many times—a sexblinded, copper-plated fool not the least of them—but he'd never once considered crossing the trail to the other side of law and order even for a cunning, pretty-titted temptress.

Not once. He just hadn't been written up that way, and he knew he never would be.

"Rest your vocal cords, Danielle," he told the girl as, holding the barrel of his .44 against her flat belly, he leaned toward her, hooked her cartridge belt with his boot, and dragged it back away from her. She kept her brash, wistful gaze on him, and he could see the wheels of escape turning in her head.

He glanced at Cousin Wilbur. "Lieutenant, be a good outlaw and kick your gunbelt over here. Then you both lay down flat on your bellies, hands behind your backs."

The wounded, suited gent continued to sob and groan, breathing hard and muttering prayers for forgiveness.

"Hush, Waco," Danielle barked. "If there is a God in Heaven, he sure as shit ain't gonna listen to you. You're goin' straight to the Devil's fryin' pan for all eternity. So why don't you just die and give us all a little break here, huh?"

Waco spit a glob of blood into the bunchgrass and cried, "Shut the fuck up, you bitch! It was your idea to come up here anyways, Danielle!" More blood dribbled over his lips and down his chin. "We was doin' all right down in Arkansas. But, no, you had to come up here and get in on *this* action. And now look what happened." He slumped down on his shoulder, blinking slowly. "This fuckin' lawdog kilt me 'cause Wilbur wouldn't let us kill him . . . back . . . back in the. . . ."

He sighed, and his head dropped like a rock. He was dead.

"Thank Christ," Wilbur said, belly down on the ground, arms behind his back. "As if my nerves ain't shot enough already!"

Longarm checked Wilbur and Danielle for hideout weapons, finding one peashooter on each, one knife on Wilbur, and two wicked-looking little stilettos on Danielle, one hanging in a sheath between her lightly freckled breasts and another snugged into a second sheath stitched to the inside of her boot.

"Damn," he said with a chuckle, tossing both stilettos into the brush. "I bet you spit poison."

"You know what my spit tastes like, lawdog," Danielle said mockingly, lifting her chin above the gravel and sage. "Didn't hear you complainin' none."

"You both stay there—still as statues," Longarm said as he tramped off to fetch rope from their saddles.

When he had them both tied—wrists as well as ankles—
he unsaddled two of their horses and turned them loose. He
strapped the strongbox to the packhorse, then brought two
horses over to Danielle and Wilbur, untying their ankles
long enough for each to mount up.

"What about Waco and the others?" Wilbur asked.
"Ain't you gonna bury 'em?"

"Why go to all that trouble?" Longarm said. "The crit-
ters'll have 'em taken care of in a couple days. If you wanna
say some nice words over 'em, though, Wilbur—I ain't
gonna stop ya."

When he had their wrists tied to their saddle horns, and
their ankles tied to their stirrups, Longarm mounted the
spare saddle horse, and leading the packhorse and the horses
of the outlaw cousins, headed back up to where his steeldust waited behind the rocky ridge.

He stepped down from the spare horse, and removed the
mount's saddle, bridle, bedroll, and saddlebags. Then he
slapped the horse's rump, and it hightailed off to the south,
snorting and kicking.

"Fine horseflesh," he told Wilbur and Danielle, who
were sitting their saddles looking glum and angry, though
Wilbur also looked relieved. Outlawing had obviously taken
its toll on the handsome young man's nerves. Some, like
Danielle, were cut out for it. Some weren't. "You bring them
all the way up from Arkansas?"

As Longarm dug his rye bottle out of his saddlebags,
Danielle told him to diddle himself. "Don't tell him a damn
thing, Wilbur," she ordered, cutting her fierce eyes at her
cousin. "Don't give him the satisfaction."

Wilbur only chuffed and shook his head. His dark brown
hair hung in his eyes as he turned to Longarm, who'd hiked
a hip on a rock to rest and imbibe in some rye for his ach-

ing noggin. "We came up from Arkansas when we heard about the gold being robbed regularly from the Clark & Kinney Line."

Longarm threw back a second shot from the bottle and furrowed a curious brow at the handsome young gent. "You two wouldn't be the ones who tried to have me bushwhacked in Rabbit Ridge, would you?"

Wilbur looked at Danielle. She looked hard at first, defiant. But then a wry little smile quirked her thin but kissable lips. She turned to Longarm.

"Sure."

"Those two shooters part of your gang?"

"Sure," Danielle repeated. "They'd just thrown in with us. Thanks for proving ole Roy and Ray didn't have the mettle."

Longarm's frown deepened. "What about Arizona?"

"We just hired her to 'occupy' you while Roy and Ray did the dirty work." She smiled with even more delight.

"I'll be goddamned," Longarm muttered, genuinely indignant.

That damn Arizona . . .

The lawman said, "So Plan B was last night?"

Wilbur hiked a shoulder. "That was the original plan. Roy and Ray's ambush was just a spur-o'-the-moment idea— after too much whiskey, I reckon. We knew the driver and shotgun rider would be looking for a whole gang, not a cavalry officer and his pretty wife." He glanced at Danielle, who continued to smile mockingly at Longarm. "And when we learned the robbers weren't hitting the line until three days out from Rabbit Ridge . . ."

"We figured we'd hit it two days out, when everyone would be off their guard," Danielle said. "And when it would be easy to . . . uh . . . distract the shotgun rider until one of my boys came up behind him and tapped him on his fool head."

Longarm threw back another drink, enjoyed the burn as it went down and the medicinal fuzz it cast up over his brain, soothing the tortured nerve ends and easing the ringing in his ears.

He chuckled dryly. "Well, I sure walked into that one. But you two walked into it now. I'll be turnin' you over to the law at Crow Canyon. Hope you don't have any outstanding warrants from down Arkansas way—for murder, say. Hate to see such a pretty couple swing."

Wilbur blew out a sigh and hung his head. "Oh, Lordy!"

"Shut up, you damn sissy!" Danielle snarled.

Wilbur shook his hanging head. His lips bunched below the thick, dark brown curls dangling over the man's face, and Longarm thought he heard him sob.

Danielle shot a fiery look at Longarm. "This is getting embarrassing. Wilbur's killed as many as anyone in our whole gang—when we had a gang; left most of the homebodies in the Ozarks—and now look at him, cryin' like a baby at the prospect of the hang rope. Wicked Wilbur, they called him down along the Cimarron. Shot two Rangers and a deputy sheriff in Kansas during one robbery alone!"

Wilbur jerked his red, wet face at his cousin. "Shut up, Danielle. I don't wanna die!"

Danielle only laughed and kept her mocking eyes on Longarm. "Now he's suddenly become Weepin' Wilbur! Come on, Marshal." She jerked back and forth in her saddle. "Let's get this show on the road! This is just too damn embarrassing. I can't take it anymore!"

The ride back toward the stage station was uneventful until, about halfway there, Longarm heard the rataplan of many galloping hooves. The thuds seemed to emanate from a canyon cut into the base of the mountain slope he and the outlaw cousins were riding across.

He pulled his horse, the packhorse, and the horses of Wilbur and Danielle back behind a pile of rock that had tumbled from the ridge above him, and tied all four mounts to shrubs. Then he shucked his Winchester from his saddle boot and rammed a round into the chamber.

"What the hell is that?" Wilbur asked. "Sounds like a good dozen riders movin' fast."

"I don't know," Longarm said. "You and your cuz sit tight while I check it out."

"You can't leave us here trussed up like this!" Danielle admonished. "What if you get yourself greased by a band of desperadoes? We'll *rot* up here!"

Longarm glanced at the girl. His impatience with the deadly little she-viper must have shone on his face. Wilbur turned to her and said, "Shut up, Danielle," and for the first time that morning, she had nothing to say. She just gave a slow, indignant blink, and stared at her horse's mane.

Holding his rifle in both hands across his chest, Longarm tramped out from behind the rocks and sort of side-stepped down the steep slope. As he continued toward the lip of the canyon that opened below, the drumbeats of the horses grew louder.

He dropped to his hands and knees and crawled the last twenty feet to the canyon's lip, hearing the rattle of tack and the snorting of several winded mounts.

He'd no sooner gotten down behind some rocks lining the lip of the canyon than a rider—a potbellied gent with a gray sombrero, pink neckerchief, and crisscrossed bandoliers on his chest—galloped around the bend in the canyon wall to his right.

Several more riders followed, riding tall in the saddle, reins slack in their gloved hands. They were all dusty, sweat-stained, bearded, and armed for bear. Cartridge casings from many bandoliers flashed in the mid-morning sun. So did silver-chased six-shooters and the brass receivers of Winchester and Henry rifles. Longarm even caught the flash of a silver tooth.

The lawman watched from a narrow crack between the rocks as the riders passed through the narrow, winding defile before him, the reports of their mounts' shod hooves echoing off the chalky walls.

Dust rose, peppering Longarm's eyes and nostrils.

When the last man in the party had disappeared with the others behind another bend to Longarm's left, the lawman had counted an even ten riders. He lifted a hand from his Winchester's front stock to pensively scratch the two-day stubble on his anvil jaws.

More hoof clomps rose from his right.

He quickly lowered his head again, and peeked through the gap in the rocks to see another rider—a scrawny towheaded kid in a wolf vest—walk a pinto pony out from around the leftward bend in the canyon wall, following the others. The kid couldn't have been much over seventeen, if he was even that, though he lazed back in his saddle, his right leg hooked over his saddle horn as he whittled away at a chunk of wood in his hands with a pocketknife.

The shavings from the half-carved figure arced out into the sunlight, littering the rocks and finely ground dust of the canyon floor.

The kid wore a sun-faded bowler hat. His eyes were small and pinched, giving him an arrogant, devilish air, but his face was pale and soft as a baby's ass. The sunlight betrayed a few blond sprouts of a fledgling mustache, and an equally inept attempt at sideburns. But what caught the brunt of Longarm's attention was the big rifle snugged down in the rifle boot under the kid's left thigh. It was wide and long, with a massive brass butt plate.

A Big Fifty buffalo gun, like the one Anderson had mentioned the sharpshooter carried.

As the kid's horse turned to slowly follow the bend out away from Longarm, Longarm caught a glimpse of what could only have been a tripod for the long gun dangling from the saddle's right side.

The leisurely *snick-snicks* of the kid's knife dwindled along with the clomps of his slow-moving horse, and horse and rider disappeared behind the curving canyon wall. Chalky dust sifted. There was one more clomp as the horse's shod hoof kicked a stone, then silence.

Slowly, when he was sure no more riders were coming, Longarm stood. He stared after the kid, remembering the Big Fifty filling the kid's saddle boot.

"Ain't no buffalo out here, boy," Longarm said, running his tongue along his lower lip. "So, what're you huntin' with that cannon?"

Longarm turned and began tramping up toward the rocks where his prisoners waited, answering his own question.

"Me, that's who."

Chapter 15

"It's him!" Rye Spurlock yelled. *"It's him! It's him!"*

Leading his prisoners up along the corral east of the barn, under a sun that was nearly straight up in the sky, Longarm saw the girl run off the porch, where the two cowboys and the gambler sat around a barrel, playing cards.

The stage sat in the middle of the yard. It was aimed west, though the horses were not yet in the hitch. Rye stopped at the rear of the coach and, hand on a hip, watched with apprehensive eyes as Longarm, the outlaw cousins, and the bullion-bearing packhorse rode up.

"Well, I'll be goddamned," Johnny Anderson said, coming out of the cabin with a cup of coffee in one hand, a cigar in the other. His long duster flapped about the tops of his tall boots. "You run 'em to ground, didja, Gus? Or whatever the hell your name is," the jehu added as he stepped off the porch and sauntered over to where Longarm was now dismounting.

"Call me Longarm," the lawman said, heading back to cut his prisoners free of their saddles. "And if you wanna get the strongbox off that packhorse, I'll go ahead and make my prisoners comfortable in the coach, and then we can salt some sage."

"My, my, my," Anderson said, staring up at the cousins, incredulous. "I never woulda figured those two for stage robbers."

"Me neither," Longarm muttered with some chagrin as he cut Danielle's wrists free of her saddle horn.

"How in the hell did they get the bullion," Anderson pressed, "if you—a federal lawman, was . . . ?"

He let his voice trail off as Longarm turned to him, ice in the lawman's brown eyes.

"Ah, well, never mind about that," Anderson said, narrowing one eye at Danielle in speculation.

Rubbing a hand across his bearded face, he glanced at the big half-breed, the two old hostlers, and the string-bean kid, who were tramping across the yard from the barn, the little yellow dog once again nipping with savage playfulness at the string bean's heels. "Tommy-John, get over here and help me load the strongbox onto the stage," Anderson barked. "Goddamnit, I got a timetable to keep!"

They were ready to roll inside of fifteen minutes. As Longarm and Johnny Anderson climbed up into the driver's box, the swing station's old matriarch, Miss Willa, hoisted herself out of her wicker chair on the porch, where she'd stonily overseen the hitching of the horses and the securing of the strongbox.

Having the box stolen out of her station had, judging by her pursed lips and flat-eyed stare, been rather hard on the proud old gal's heart. As Anderson whipped the team out of the yard, Longarm, glancing over his shoulder through the dust lifting from the churning wheels, thought he saw the woman lower her shoulders with a relieved sigh and give a fateful shake of her head.

She doubtless held out little hope of the bullion safely making it to Crow Canyon. And remembering the group of obvious thieves and killers he'd seen riding through the canyon earlier, Longarm wasn't so sure himself.

One thing he did know, however, was that no woman was going to catch him with his pants down again. Not until they'd made it through Demon Rock Canyon, that is, and had pulled safely into Crow Canyon on the far side of the Continental Divide. If he survived this trip, which was looking less and less likely, he'd probably take his pants down three or four times before making the long trek back to Denver.

As the horses stretched their strides into easy lopes, he told Anderson about the well-armed long-riders.

"Well, fuck," Anderson said, "I'm getting too old for this shit. First them two you got trussed inside the coach, now those wolves again. I don't think my ticker can take the stress of this kinda work no more. I had an easier time fightin' old Red Cloud up the Bozeman."

"My sentiments exactly," Longarm said, digging a nickel cheroot from an inside pocket of his corduroy coat. He scratched a match to life on his holster and, balancing the big coach gun across high thighs, cupped the flame around the end of his cigar, puffing smoke. "If I keep gettin' sent out on assignments like this one, I'm liable to retire and head to Baja. Shack up with a pert little señorita and fish in the Sea of Cortez."

Anderson set the handle of his bullwhip in the steel socket jutting up beside the brake, and sat up straight in the seat, the team's ribbons resting lightly in his practiced hands. "Got a nest egg, do ya, Longarm?"

Longarm let the wind take a breath of exhaled smoke. "Nope."

Anderson chuckled. "Me neither. Shit, I reckon I never figured I'd live this fucking long!"

They'd been in the canyon of the Demon Rock River for an hour when Longarm spied a sharp sun flash against the wall of the high, boulder-strewn ridge ahead of the stage and on the right side of the winding trail. Longarm's nerves had been sputtering and fluttering since they'd left the last stage relay station, and now he felt the hair on the back right side of his scalp tingle.

That's where he figured he'd catch the sniper's bullet when it came. Unless he could somehow get the son of a bitch first.

Holding the shotgun across his thighs, his body moving with the sway and pitch of the fast-moving coach, he stared at the spot where he'd seen the sun flash. He couldn't see much of anything except red rock and a small, dark brown patch of color against the side of the ridge.

He stared hard for a couple of minutes, but the flash did not come again.

Could be mica catching the waning afternoon sunlight, or a bottle cast off by a prospector. On the other hand, it could be the reflection off the chasing of a rifle receiver—say, the brass receiver of a Big Fifty buffalo gun.

Longarm looked behind. Then he glanced at the river that had widened out to the left of the trail, flashing behind a sparse screen of cottonwoods and aspens.

He nudged Johnny Anderson's shoulder with his elbow, then tossed his head toward the river. "Time to water the team."

Anderson looked at him, scowling. "We just watered 'em near an hour ago."

"Let's water 'em again. I'm gonna scout ahead a ways on foot."

"Goddamnit, Longarm, I gotta timetable to keep! As late as we are right now, we ain't gonna make Crow Canyon till well after dark!"

"You wanna keep your timetable *with* the bullion or without it?"

"Shit!"

Anderson pulled the team off the left side of the trail and gigged them on over to the river through a gap in the trees.

"What the hell we stoppin' for?" yelled one of the cowboys from below, drunkenly slurring his words. "Them owlhoots doggin' our asses?"

The cowboy's name was Bill Lang, Longarm had learned. He and his partner, Clem Grayson, were heading for a ranch owned by a friend of theirs out by Crow Canyon, where they'd landed work manning a remote line shack.

Their gambling friend was one Hannibal Jenkins, a lush who spoke with a thick English accent and shared his liquor freely with Lang and Grayson. Both old cowboys seemed to be making up in advance for a long, cold mountain winter likely with a short ration of tanglefoot.

"Longarm!" Rye yelled from the opposite side of the coach. "It ain't Cormorant, is it?"

"No, it ain't Cormorant. No, it ain't nobody," Longarm yelled.

"Then why are we stopping?" asked the gambler when Anderson had stopped the team about twenty yards from the stream and all the passengers except for the tied cousins had climbed out. The gambler pinched the upswept corners of his handlebar mustache, shifting his weight around unsteadily, his breath smelling like a brandy barrel. "I paid

good money for a seat on this crate, and I don't appreci-
ate . . ."

The man let his voice trail off as Longarm favored him
with another icy stare. When the gambler had wandered off,
grumbling with the two cowboys, who'd started building
brown-paper quirleys, Longarm swung the coach gun over
his shoulder.

"What're you gonna do, Longarm?" Rye asked.

"Gonna hoof it up trail a ways," Longarm said, making
sure all the lanyard's bandolier loops were filled. "You sit
tight, Miss Rye. Stick close to Johnny. He'll protect you if
ole Cormorant comes a-limpin' anywhere within rifle
range."

Longarm winked at the driver, who was adjusting the
hame on one of the horses, then glanced into the stage at
Danielle and Wilbur, sitting side by side with their wrists
and ankles tied. Their faces were caked with trail dust.

"I gotta pee," Danielle growled, curling her upper lip.

"Hold it," Longarm told her, walking back through the
still-sifting dust toward the old army freight trail they'd
been following.

"Fuckin' bastard!" Danielle called behind him.

"He's not a bastard," Rye said in Longarm's defense,
glowering into the stage. "You're a thief and a no-good
charlatan! And who does your chicken-shit cousin think he
is—masqueradin' as an army man. Ha! I pegged you both
for scoundrels way back in Rabbit Ridge!"

Danielle complimented Rye in turn, though Longarm
was too far away now to hear the no-doubt grisly details.
He chose a well-covered spot to cross the trail, out of sight
from the northern ridge, then broke into a jog to the ridge's
boulder-strewn base.

Drawing a deep breath, he began climbing the ridge, angling around the boulders and stunted firs and cedars as he made his way toward the brown spot about halfway up the slope and a good three hundred yards farther west.

When he'd climbed for fifteen minutes, the altitude making his heart flutter and his head light, he stopped for a breather. Behind and below, the stage was little larger than a red and yellow matchbox. Johnny Anderson had un-hitched the team and led them over to the stream, while the passengers milled around in the trees—no larger than stick figures from this distance.

Cursing himself for the cigar habit that had shrunk his lungs, Longarm continued a little farther up the slope, then, halfway between the top and bottom of the ridge, followed a prospector's burro or mule trail west. He continued around a broad knob jutting out into the canyon, then stopped sud-denly, stepping back under an overhanging stone ledge and dropping to one knee.

Directly below him, thirty yards away, a mine shaft jut-ted straight out from the ridge wall. At the very end of the timbered roof, which was littered with rocks and gravel fallen from above, stood the kid whom Longarm had seen following the trail wolves through the canyon earlier. The kid stood looking back toward the stage, the Big Fifty cra-dled in his arms, the tripod setup nearby.

Longarm could see only the kid's profile from this an-gle, but the towheaded younker appeared to be scowling. Smoke from the loosely rolled quirley dangling between his lips puffed around his shabby bowler hat. The octagonal barrel of the long gun in his arms caught the coppery light occasionally in spite of the kid's attempt to keep the brass receiver shielded with his arm.

Longarm stretched a wolfish smile and dropped the barn blaster's front stock into the palm of his right hand, slowly, gently earing back the hammers. The rest of the gang might be near, so he didn't want to use the gun, but he'd blow the kid into the next century if he had to.

"Come on, goddamnit—what's keepin' you stupid sonso'bitches?" he heard the kid mutter as the little owlhoot stared toward the stage, which was barely visible from here.

The trail passed nearly directly below the kid's position so that when the stage passed, the pinch-faced sharpshooter would have had a devastatingly clean shot at the shotgun guard.

Longarm hunkered low, wincing, hoping the kid didn't sense his presence and turn toward him. His muscles loosened with relief as the kid turned in the opposite direction, then, muttering something Longarm couldn't hear, sat down, crossed his legs, and set the big rifle across his thighs.

The kid picked up the small carving and the folding knife. As he began hacking away at the wooden figure, continuing to mutter angrily as he sent shavings flying out around him, Longarm straightened and, with painstaking slowness, crept down the slope toward the roof of the mine shaft.

Snick, snick went the knife, which the kid wielded with angry impatience.

Longarm set one boot below the other, careful not to loose any gravel in his wake, squeezing the shotgun in both his gloved hands. He tried to make each step coincide with the harsh scrape of the kid's knife. Occasionally, he looked around to be sure no other gang members were near. They were likely farther up the trail, waiting to swarm the stage when the shotgun rider had been blown out of the driver's boot.

Longarm closed on the kid.

The kid's back faced him, his shoulders jerking as he worked, occasional muttered oaths rising to Longarm's ears. Longarm kept a close eye on his own shadow angling out to his left and, fortunately, behind him and beyond the field of the kid's peripheral vision.

When he could see the individual hairs in the kid's ragged wolf vest, he set both barrels of the gut shredder against the kid's sun-reddened neck, just below the line of his short, sandy blond hair. Feeling the cool iron barrels pressing against his skin, the kid turned to stone.

Longarm said, "Just set that elephant stopper on the ground in front of you, Junior. Consider that you have two eight-gauge cannons kissing your neck, that both hammers are cocked full back, and that my trigger finger's given to the palsy!"

Chapter 16

After a stretched second during which he contemplated only the Devil knows what, the sharpshooting younker said, "Fuck." With both hands, he lifted the Big Fifty up off his lap and set it on the ground in front of his crossed legs.

"Who the hell're you?" he asked tightly, raising his hands shoulder high.

Longarm reached forward and slipped the kid's six-shooter from his holster. "The man whose head you were fixin' to blow off with that big popper of yours, you scrawny little backshootin' son of a bitch!" With that, he grabbed the kid's pistol by its barrel and raked the butt over the kid's head, denting one side of his bowler hat.

"Ouch!" the kid yelped, covering his head and glancing over his shoulder at Longarm. "That hurt, ya big ape!"

Longarm tossed the kid's pistol into the canyon. He kicked the kid belly down atop the mine shaft roof and slipped a short, rusty knife from a sheath dangling from the back of the kid's cartridge belt. He tossed the knife after the pistol as the kid glanced over his shoulder once more, his eyes pinched with incredulity and anger. "You're the shot-gun guard?"

"You're smarter than you look, you little fuck."

"But . . . but . . ." the kid sputtered.

"Shut up." Longarm grabbed the kid's right foot, turned, and holding the big shotgun on his shoulder, dragged the kid back off the roof and behind a couple of wagon-sized granite boulders.

Rocks flew. The kid spit grit from his lips and cursed, futilely clawing at the ground with his bare hands.

Longarm kicked the kid into a sitting position against the back of the boulders, in a deep wedge of purple shade, well hidden from the canyon below. Dust wafted. The kid had lost his hat and his dirty hair hung in his eyes. He wore a look of savage fury.

"You son of a bitch!" he cried. "You can't—!"

Longarm buried the toe of his left cavalry boot in the kid's belly. The kid jerked forward, clutching his middle, groaning and trying to suck air into his lungs. Longarm hadn't kicked him nearly as hard as he'd wanted to.

"What's your name, boy? I'm not gonna ask you twice."

His face pinched with pain as he crouched over his bat-tered middle, the kid cast a sidelong look up at Longarm. "Who wants to know?"

"Custis P. Long, deputy U.S. marshal out of Denver."

"You're a *lawman*?"

"That's right. Now you answer my question or you're gonna get a whole lot more pain than what you're experi-encin' now."

"Charley Dodd, for chrissakes!" the kid barked, sucking another sharp breath down his throat.

"From where?"

"Montana."

"That where the others are from?"

"Shit, I don't know where they're from. Here and there, I reckon. You don't sit around and talk about such twaddle! We're outlaws, for chrissakes!"

"I counted eleven in the canyon earlier," Longarm said, glaring down at the gasping younker. "Did I count right?"

"That's how many's currently ridin' with us, yessir."

"Who's the leader?"

The kid swallowed, sighed, and straightened his back. "Now, you know I can't tell you that. Shit, I'd get—!"

Longarm swung the double bores of the coach gun against the kid's right temple. He caught him again on the backswing. Not hard enough to do any real damage, but enough to let the kid know who was in charge.

The kid's head jerked left to right and back again. The kid howled and mashed his fists against his temples, gritting his teeth and sobbing. "You're crazy! How'm I supposed to tell you anything if you knock my damn head off my shoulders?"

Longarm pressed the double bores against the top of the kid's head. "If there's anything I hate, it's a yellow-livered, backshootin' son of a bitch. You best tell me what I wanna know, Charley Dodd, or your shoulders are gonna look mighty funny without a head!"

"Pink! Pink Hutchins!"

"What about him?"

"He's the head honcho. Him and his brother Vernon. Now, quit abusin' me, dang-it. I may not be the sharpest tool in the shed, but I know it ain't right, you knockin' me around like this."

"I'm gonna take you back to the *real* school of hard knocks, Charley, if you don't answer one more real quick-like."

His face a mask of dread and desperation, young Charley Dodd looked up at Longarm between the fists he'd mashed against his beet red temples. "What's that?"

"Where they fixin' to hit the stage?"

"Ah, shit—that's an easy one."

Longarm mashed the shotgun barrels down harder against the kid's head.

"I don't know!" the kid squealed. "I don't know, I tell ya. They didn't tell me. My job's to knock off the shotgun man—that's all. All I know is where Pink and Vernon want me to shoot the son of a . . . uh . . . excuse me—I mean the poor defenseless hombre. The rest is up to them and the rest of the gang." Dodd lifted an eye to Longarm. "I can give ya my best guess, though."

Longarm stared down at the kid, his mouth a knife slash beneath his longhorn mustache.

"Somewhere up the trail a ways!" the kid said, unable to keep a smile from lifting his mouth corners. Immediately, he dropped his head to his crossed arms, cowering and begging for mercy.

"All right," Longarm said, leaning his shotgun against a gravelly shelf behind him and extracting the two sets of handcuffs from his coat pockets. "Turn around, weasel."

"What're you gonna do?"

"Cuff you till I've got your gang in hand and can come back for you."

The kid's eyes widened in exasperation. "What happens if you don't come back?"

"Then you'll make some bobcat or grizzly bear mighty happy, I reckon. That's about all you're good for anyway, you fork-tailed demon."

The kid kicked and squealed like a three-year-old with a temper tantrum. "I got rights!"

"Ah, shit," Longarm said. He was done fooling with the kid. He had a gang to run down.

If they didn't run him down first . . .

With that he grabbed his shotgun and, swinging its heavy stock like a club, laid the kid out flat against the base of the boulder. Out like a hurricane lamp in a sudden gale.

Longarm trussed him up like a hog for the slaughter, using the kid's own neckerchief to gag him, then retraced his steps back down the mountain to where the stage waited by the river.

As Longarm approached the Concord, Rye Spurlock was waiting for him at the rear luggage boot. Her eyes shone nearly as much white as those almost phosphorescent brown irises of hers, and her breasts lifted with edginess. "You didn't see Cormorant out there, didja, Longarm?"

"Miss Rye," the lawman said, brushing past her toward where Johnny Anderson was hitching the team to the coach, "we got bigger fish to fry than Weed Cormorant."

"No one's bigger fry than Cormorant!" she snapped at his back.

"Anything out there, Marshal?" asked the gambler, Hannibal Jenkins.

He was walking, half-staggering up from the trees, puffing a long, slim black cigar, the tail of his long, green neckerchief wafting in the afternoon breeze. He had a light red mustache and goatee, and he wore a bullet-crowned, flat-brimmed black hat. A worn box of playing cards was wedged behind the hat's elastic band.

The two cowboys, Lang and Grayson, flanked him.

"One owlhoot down," Longarm told him. "About ten more to go, if my math is right." He glanced at the glassy-eyed cowboys and at Johnny Anderson, who straightened from the double-tree hitch, wincing and clapping an arm across his lower back. "The sniper's done been put to sleep, but we're gonna get hit," Longarm added. "About all we can do is prepare ourselves and hope we take the main group by surprise, get past 'em before they know we're comin'. Unless I've missed my guess, the sniper's rifle report is their signal to leather up and ride. Without the rifle shot, we might catch 'em with their pants down."

"Ah, shit—just our luck, Clem," Bill Lang complained to his partner. "First stage I took in six years is the one that gets struck by long-riders."

"You always been bad luck for me, Bill," Clem said, and belched. "If we git through this, I might have to git shed of you."

As Bill cursed his partner, the gambler took one more step toward Longarm, shucking his Colt Sheriff's model from the cross-draw holster high on his left hip. "When the time comes, Marshal Long," he said, opening the pistol's loading gate and narrowing a green eye at the chambers as he slowly rolled the cylinder, "rest assured I'm quite handy with this little equalizer here, and that your play will be duly backed."

"Count me in on that," Bill Lang said with a nod, blowing his sour whiskey breath. "This asshole Clem an' me done tussled with our share of long-loopers on the Panhandle. We'll give them long-riders something' to think about, they try stoppin' *this* coach!"

With that, he rapped a fist against the Concord's side panel, and gave Longarm a resolute wink and a nod.

For his part, Clem just glowered at his partner, shaking his head.

"'Preciate the help, fellas," said Longarm. "And with ten men on the other side, I'll likely need help. But I suggest you go easy on the hooch from here on in. Wouldn't want you ventilatin' each other."

"Or me," Rye chuffed, flanking Longarm on his left.

"Or Miss Rye here," Longarm agreed. "Johnny, you ready to go?"

"No," Anderson grumbled. "But the horses are, so let's get this consarned show on the road."

Anderson gave the team's tack one more quick check. Then, as the passengers climbed aboard the rocking coach and Longarm closed and latched the door behind them, the driver climbed wearily into the Concord's hurricane deck. Walking around to the other side, Longarm climbed aboard as well, and then Anderson hoorawed the team back through the trees to the main trail, and hung a left.

A few minutes later, he had the team loping toward the hulking blue mass of the Demon Rock Pass looming ahead, above the fluttering golden leaves of the Demon Rock River.

The trail generally followed the river, which was low this time of the year. The canyon's walls drew back from the trail and the stream, then closed again, and Longarm studied the ridges, the occasional sparse aspen copses, and the boulders that had fallen from the canyon walls— anywhere the gang might be holed up and awaiting the signal of Charley Dodd's Big Fifty.

Anderson rode silently, his heavy, slouched frame jerking with the stage's rocks and lurches. Ordinarily, he leaned forward with his elbows on his knees. Now, however, the old jehu sat straight-backed, scouring both sides of the trail as carefully as Longarm did, his leathery eye lids narrowed over blue eyes that were shaded by the down-canted brim of his weather-stained hat.

He kept his spruce green duster tucked back behind the

Remington .44 holstered on his right hip. The keeper thong hung free of the hammer. His Henry repeater leaned against his thigh.

Neither Anderson nor Longarm said anything. No one in the coach seemed to be conversing either.

The only sounds were the team's clomping hooves, the horses' occasional snorts, the squawk of the stage's thoroughbraces, and the low rush of the river when the trail angled close to the bank. Five minutes after taking to the trail once more, Longarm watched the sun crest the pass straight ahead of the stage and heavy shadows bleed out from the mountain wall, softening the glow of the yellow leaves to his left.

It was an eerie, brooding light. And the silence was heavy and ominous, drawing the muscles taut between the lawman's shoulder blades.

Left of the trail, something screamed suddenly, raucously. Anderson jerked with a start, and Longarm brought the shotgun up.

Both men froze as a crow, continuing to send its angry cries echoing around the canyon, and lighting from a big ash tree on the trail's left side, flapped its wings toward the darkening bulk of the pass hulking straight ahead.

Anderson and Longarm shared a tense glance. Then the old driver's eyes widened as his gaze angled over Longarm's right shoulder, toward the trail's right side.

Longarm jerked his head in the same direction, tightening his grip on the shotgun. White smoke rose from a thin aspen copse about fifty yards from the trail, billowing nearly straight up above the trees. A dozen or so horses were tied to a picket line at the edge of the copse, facing the woods, and near the horses, a man stood looking toward the trail.

From that distance and in the dulling light, the man was little more than a hatted silhouette. But Longarm caught the reflection of wan sunlight off the cartridge-filled bandoliers crisscrossing his chest.

The man held one hand up against the westering sun angling down from the pass, and then he turned his head sharply to one side and shouted something Longarm could barely make out above the team's clomps and the stage's clatter but that could only have been: *"The stage!"*

Longarm shot a quick look at Anderson and, bringing up the coach gun, snarled, "This is it—step 'em up, hoss!"

Chapter 17

"Jesus Christ, you're gonna turn this bloody thing over!" the Brit gambler yelled in the coach beneath Longarm as they all hammered along the trail, fishtailing around bends.

The driver continued to harangue the team and pop the blacksnake over the horses' backs.

In the meantime, the first three riders had drawn within fifty yards of the stage and were closing fast, as the stage horses were blowing out quickly on the long rise toward the pass looming ahead. As the cowboys and the gambler snapped off shots from the windows on both sides of the coach—wild shots, that is, for the stage was pitching around too violently for even halfway accurate shooting—Longarm thumbed the coach gun's rabbit-eared hammers back to full cock.

He rested the ends of the double barrels on the brass rail running along the back of the coach's roof.

The three riders ate up the trail behind him, two firing Winchesters while the third snapped off revolver shots, their smoke puffs dancing on the wind. Several slugs smacked into the back of the coach with angry cracks, or ricochetted off the churning wheels with raucous pings. But most blew up dust on either side of the trail.

A long, straggly line of riders snaked out a good distance behind the three, disappearing occasionally behind hills or around the slight bends in the steadily climbing freight road.

Longarm crouched low, snugged his cheek against the two-bore's rear stock, and firmed up his right index finger on the trigger.

Off the end of the barrel, the three near riders pitched, bobbed, and swayed above the laid-back ears of their horses' heads. One man lost his hat on the wind, then leaned low to coax more speed from his white-socked black. Smoke and flames stabbed from the barrel of the man's Smith & Wesson .44.

The slug screamed past Longarm's right cheek. He could feel its heat against his ear.

Longarm squeezed the shotgun's left hammer.

BOOM!

The pistol-wielding rider jerked back in his saddle as his blue shirt blew open under his black vest. Blood exploded from the gaping hole in his chest. He fired off one more round skyward as he screamed and did a backward somersault off his lunging horse's ass.

He'd been the middle rider. As his riderless horse swerved in front of another galloping outlaw, cutting him off, Longarm shifted the shotgun to the third man, and squeezed the trigger.

The gun leaped and kicked back savagely against Longarm's shoulder. It turned the third rider into a headless horseman for about five seconds, before the man's headless body, firing its Winchester into the trail beneath him, sagged down its galloping, screaming horse's left hip.

Spraying blood from the ragged hole atop its shoulders, the corpse rolled and bounced along the trail, to be trampled seconds later by several more riders moving up from behind.

"Holy shit in the parson's thunder mug!" someone roared in the coach below Longarm. "I see now why they've been takin' the shotgun rider to the dance first!"

Quickly, Longarm breeched the big popper, twisted out the spent wads, and inserted fresh. He snapped the shotgun closed and hunkered down once more.

He slackened his trigger finger. Only a few riders were continuing to gallop toward him—one angling off the trail's left side and apparently trying to get around him. The main group held back around the bodies of the two dead men, holding their reins high up under their chins and looking warily down and around the trail, stunned.

As one of the continuing pursuers drew within forty yards, galloping along behind a thin stand of fir trees while holding his reins in his teeth, one of the passengers fired out the coach door, snapping branches. The outlaw continued working his way parallel with the left-side stage door, his tack squawking, his horse lunging spryly.

The cowboys and the gambler were yelling curses as they continued firing, hitting only branches and pine cones.

Longarm angled the big shotgun off the gunman's side of the coach. The man, whose long bib beard buffeted in the wind, was still too far away for the gut shredder to be much use, but Longarm might at least give the man a few steel bumblebees to think about.

The lawman eared both hammers back and slid the bores

toward the rider, galloping behind the trees on a big brown and white pinto. Longarm took up the slack in his trigger finger. The rider disappeared behind a large pine tree.

There was a loud grunt and a cracking sound, and only the horse galloped out from behind tree.

Longarm eased the tension in his finger as the rider suddenly appeared from behind the tree in midair, did a violent backward flip, and hit the ground with a loud, crunching *thump!*

Longarm heard Rye Spurlock cry, "The stupid bastard was felled by a tree branch!"

The men in the coach roared with laughter and snapped a couple more obligatory shots through the pines.

Longarm slid the shotgun's bores toward the coach's backtrail, where the other two pursuers, apparently also having second thoughts about their current mission, pulled back on their horses' reins. As the stage continued plodding up the grade toward the pass at a fast walk, both men dwindled into the dusty distance.

As Longarm kept his eyes peeled and the shotgun's hammers eared back, the stage topped the pass and started down the other side.

Longarm saw only the hill behind him sheathed in shelving rock and fir trees, and the towering peaks of the pass shouldering against the dimming sky.

"Christalmighty," Johnny Anderson barked as he jerked a quick look behind. "Where the hell are they? Don't tell me that mountain leveler of yourn discouraged 'em!"

"Maybe for the time bein'," Longarm mused aloud, staring along their backtrail. Turning toward the jehu, who was also nervously scouring the pass, his beard dusty and sweat-matted, he said, "Where's the next swing station . . . ?"

Longarm let his voice trail off when a few log buildings appeared in the broad valley below and before the stage, on the left side of the trail. There was a large lip of rock jutting up from the valley floor, beneath the high southern ridge and near the river draining this side of the divide. The stage station hunkered beneath the formation—a forlorn-looking collection of shacks and corrals set on a dusty, wheel- and hoof-packed yard surrounded by clay-colored boulders, stunt cedars, and junipers.

"They ain't exac'ly set up for overnighters here, but it's too damn dark to continue on to Crow Canyon," Anderson growled.

The place was burnished copper and salmon by the setting sun, and a chill breeze tossed tumbleweeds this way and that. Smoke lifted from the roof of the wood-frame and adobe brick cabin. Besides the stage horses milling in one of the corrals, there was no movement.

"Jackrabbit Station," Anderson said, pointing a gloved finger. "Don't look like much, but its ramrod, Curly Jim Hamer, is as good with a long gun as any I know. Became a crack shot in Texas as a kid, fightin' in them feuds they had down there after the War, and then in the frontier army fightin' Injuns on the Bozeman Trail."

"Pull us in, Johnny." Hunkered down atop the stage, Longarm kept his eyes peeled on the saddleback ridge over which the trail rose and disappeared behind them. "Let's get the strongbox secured before we do anything with the horses."

"Got a little better place for the strongbox here than we did at the Hawk Ridge Station." Anderson chuckled, giving Longarm a wry sidelong glance as he pulled the team off the trail and hoorawed it toward the station buildings.

"Curly Jim's got him a root cellar in his kitchen, with one hell of a squeaky trapdoor!"

"Nice to know," Longarm grumbled as he stared over the shotgun's double barrels toward the ridge, where nothing moved except a couple of swirling, copper-colored dust devils.

He wanted to believe the cutthroats had lost their money lust in the bloodshed on the other side of the pass. But it wasn't likely. They were a savage pack of bloodthirsty, money-hungry wolves, and they wouldn't give up the fight until they had the strongbox, or were turned toe down attempting to get it.

They'd likely make another try after good dark, or at first light tomorrow morning.

The weary, lathered horses blew as Anderson urged them across a wooden bridge over the narrow, willow-sheathed river, past the corral where the fresh horses bugled greetings, and into the yard under the overhanging rock.

Longarm heard the cabin's door latch click, and turned his head away from the shotgun to see a tall, gaunt, gray-bearded gent in coveralls and a beaded, deerskin vest emerge from the shack, holding a Henry rifle in both hands across his thighs. He wore a martin hat high on his thin, curly, gray curls, and he narrowed his brown eyes at the stage.

"I heard the shootin' on the other side of the pass," he said grimly. "Figured it was you. Hafta say I'm right surprised your shotgun rider's still wearin' his hat."

"Oh, it's them gun wolves that lost their hats," Anderson said, setting the brake as the team settled into its traces before the cabin. "Leastways, one of 'em did. Another's visitin' St. Peter, holdin' his ticker in both bloody hands. Ha!

The others musta taken that as an ill omen, as they gave up the chase soon after."

"They'll be back," Longarm said as, holding the coach gun in one hand, he climbed down from the stage. "Maybe soon, maybe tonight. But I'm guessin' they're right piss-burned and they'll hit us before we pull out of the station in the morning."

Longarm opened the stage door, and Rye Spurlock was the first to jump out of the coach. She wore a grin behind her pretty, dusty features, and her blond, disheveled hair hung in her eyes.

"Thanks, Gus," she said, throwing her arms around Longarm's neck and planting a lusty kiss on his cheek. "I mean Longarm. You sent three of those blue-toothed demons saddlin' clouds and ridin' off to their glories."

"Only two," Longarm corrrected.

"The other'n had him a rather nasty meetin' with a big, old fir tree," said the cowboy Bill with a laugh as he left the stage unsteadily behind Rye.

"Do believe I heard his neck break," added the gambler, following behind Bill, with Clem bringing up the rear. "Awful sound. Rather like a pistol shot heard from a fair distance. If he's not dead, he likely wishes he were."

As the gambler and the two cowboys pushed through the crude cabin's single door, Rye sidled up to Longarm, clutching his arm. "You don't think they're finished with us, Marshal?"

"Doubt it, Miss Rye. You go on inside with the others. You'll be safe there. Get yourself some vittles." Longarm gave her a slightly admonishing look, wanting none of the distractions of his previous night at the Hawk Ridge Station. "You stay inside the rest of the evening now, you hear?"

The girl blushed. "All right."

As she turned toward the cabin, she stopped suddenly and lifted her head to the stationmaster standing beside the door, holding his rifle in the crook of his right arm. "Sir, you haven't seen a black-dressed man with a wooden hand and a limp, have you?"

The stationmaster scowled down at her, narrowing one eye with incredulity. "Well . . . no . . . I don't reckon I have . . ."

"Whew!" Rye said, and flinging her dusty hair over her shoulders, tramped on through the cabin's open door.

"Who the hell's she?" the station agent asked.

"Long story," Longarm said.

"As for him," Johnny Anderson said, coming around the front of the team, beating dust from his duck trousers with his gloves and raking his gaze between Longarm and the station manager, "he's Custis Long, deputy United States marshal out of Denver. He's my shotgun rider this trip. Marshal, this is my old pard, Curly Jim Hamer."

"Pleased to know you, Mr. Hamer." Longarm shook the man's gnarled plate-sized hand. As Hamer returned the shake, studying Longarm curiously, the lawman said, "I got a couple of prisoners inside the coach. Might I find a secure place for 'em inside?"

Hamer walked over to the coach, and crouched as he peered through the open door at Danielle and Wilbur Fridley, sitting across from each other in grim silence, their tied wrists in their laps. "Well," the station manager said dubiously, "I guess you can truss 'em up to one of the ceilin' posts. I ain't exactly outfitted for a jail." He canted his head to one side as he continued staring into the stage. "What the hell'd she do? She's right purty."

"I damn near fucked the good marshal to death, Mr.

Hamer," Danielle said from inside the coach. "Maybe to-night you'll get your turn."

Anderson chuckled and ran a hand across his nose.

Hamer straightened as he turned to Longarm, a befud-dled expression on his wizened, gray-bearded features be-neath his black fur hat. "What a curious load of pilgrims."

Chapter 18

Curly Jim Hamer's wife was a sad-faced, large-breasted, full-hipped Sioux who'd had her tongue cut out by a whiskey drummer in a hiders' camp outside Bismarck, Dakota Territory.

Hamer didn't say why the poor woman had had her tongue cut out, and since it was the sort of thing you didn't ask a man to elaborate on, Longarm never knew. But while the woman kept a gamy-smelling, crude, earthen-floored cabin, she was a damn good cook. Her fire-roasted elk steaks with mashed potatoes, elk gravy, wild peas, and onions were some of the best food Longarm had ever tasted.

It was heads and shoulders above the slop one paid three dollars or more for in fancy Denver eateries with their white tablecloths, fine china, and snooty waiters.

It wouldn't have been hard to eat such a meal quickly, even if he hadn't felt his stomach snuggling his backbone. As it was, Longarm polished off his last bite of wonderfully charred meat in under ten minutes.

When he'd swabbed his plate with a chunk of crusty bread, he checked the ties of his two prisoners, Danielle and Wilbur Fridley. The "kissin' cousins," as Anderson had dubbed them—though there appeared little warmth between them—were both sitting on the floor, ankles tethered and their wrists tied to ceiling joists.

In her sexy rasp, her doe eyes glued to his with a slight ironic cast, Danielle again offered Longarm a blow job if he'd untie her.

The lawman thanked her for the offer, wryly pinching his hat brim, before deeming her and her cousin securely trussed up for the night and heading outside with his shotgun to relieve Johnny Anderson. The jehu, who'd eaten supper first while Longarm had kept an eye on the yard, had been watching the station and the surrounding terrain from atop the stagecoach parked beside the main corral.

After securing the strongbox in the cellar beneath the kitchen, they'd decided they'd take turns keeping watch all night, relieving each other every couple of hours.

"Anything?" Longarm asked Anderson as the rangy, potbellied oldster climbed down heavily from the stage.

There was only a little light left in the western sky, above the black, toothy ridges of the Mosquito Range, and coyotes were calling from the other side of the valley.

"Nothin'." Anderson dropped the last two feet to the ground with a heavy grunt, and shouldered his Henry rifle. "Think I heard a bobcat somewhere on this big rock behind us. Other than that . . ."

"Sure it was a bobcat?"

"Hell, no, I ain't sure. I ain't sure about nuthin'. Every time I hear one of the horses snort, I think it's one o' them cutthroats. Christ, I wouldn't put it past 'em to try an' burn us out sometime tonight. Probably when I'm dead asleep . . . if I can sleep, which I doubt."

"My guess is they'll wait till daylight," Longarm said,

staring out into the night that grew thicker over the broad valley, stars winking to life in the darkening sky. "If they burn us out, there's a chance they may never find the loot."

"Could hit us on the trail again."

"Or when we're loading the loot onto the stage." Crouching down beside the coach, Longarm fired a match to life on his belt buckle and touched the flame to a fresh cigar. "That's when we'll wanna be careful. Don't wanna get bushwhacked from them willows out by the creek."

"At least you put the sharpshooter out of commission."

Longarm snorted, thinking of Charley Dodd all trussed up on the side of that ridge. He was going to have one long, cold night. "I'll go back and pick up what's left of him once all this is over. The discomfort'll serve him right."

"He might be cozyin' up to a bobcat 'bout now," Anderson said with a devilish chuckle, shifting his rifle from one hand to the other as he hiked up his pants. "Anyways, you sure you don't wanna get some shut-eye, Custis? I'll stay out here and keep watch for a couple more hours. I ain't gonna be able to sleep yet anyways."

"I can't sleep either. You better go in and try."

"Shit, I'll go in and play some cards with them cowpokes and that shifty-eyed Jenkins. They're likely so plowed by now, I can earn back all the money I lost last night."

As Anderson tramped heavy-footed toward the cabin, Longarm said, "Don't let Danielle entice you into cuttin' her loose."

Anderson threw an arm out. "Shit, I don't need a blow job that bad. I can wait for them half-breed girls in Crow Canyon!"

He went in and closed the door behind him, and Longarm lifted the collar of his corduroy coat against the high-

altitude air that bore a sharp bite this time of the year. He
climbed up onto the stage and sat in the boot, shotgun
across his knees, smoking and cupping the cigar's coal in
his right palm so the glow wouldn't target him.

He sat there for a long time after he'd finished his cigar,
hearing only the breeze ruffling the willows along the creek
fifty yards away, and the muffled conversations and intermittent laughter inside the cabin.

He could hear Rye's voice in there, and he smiled. The
girl had calmed down enough to join the cowboys, the
gambler, and Johnny Anderson in poker, and she wasn't
letting Anderson get by with any "funny business."

After the voices had died in the cabin, and all the lights
except a low-burning lamp had been extinguished, Longarm crawled off the stagecoach and took a long, slow walk
along the creek. He stopped occasionally to look around
and listen.

No sounds but the softly gurgling water and the breeze
scratching the drying leaves of the willows together. Occasionally, a coyote would yip and start a yammering from an
entire pack. The cries would continue for several minutes,
and then they'd die off one by one, and the night's deep,
eerie silence would descend once again.

Longarm stared toward the pass hulking up blackly in
the east, against a million twinkling stars. "Where are you
sonso'bitches?"

Maybe they wouldn't attack. Maybe they'd wait for the
next bullion run.

That would be fine with Longarm. He'd see to the safety
of the passengers by accompanying the stage the rest of the
way to Crow Canyon. There he'd secure a horse, then ride
back out here and track the murdering thieves alone. Their
number had been shaved to seven—a manageable pack

when the stalker owned the element of surprise. Likely, they wouldn't expect one man to shadow their trail, and they likely wouldn't stray far from the main freight road.

He'd have them on a short leash or dead in a few days.

Then again, that they'd give up so easily was a long shot. He couldn't help imagining them crawling around, armed to the teeth, in the wolf willows that jostled menacingly before him in the night breeze, reflected starlight flickering off their leaves.

He continued upstream, meandered back behind the canyon as far as the wave-shaped ridge, then descended the slope to the yard and climbed back aboard the stage. Soon, the cabin door latch clicked, and Longarm turned to see the tall, stooped figure of Johnny Anderson emerge, his rifle drooping from the crook of his right arm.

The jehu crossed the yard, his boot thumps sounding inordinately loud in the quiet night. He paused to let some blown weeds and a tumbleweed pass, then continued to the Concord and shoved his hat back on his head as he looked up at Longarm.

"You still kickin'?"

"So far." Longarm yawned, ran a hand down his face, and started climbing down from the boot, holding the shotgun in one hand. "How was poker?"

"Clem fleeced us all, but that girl's wilier than she looks. Accused me of cheatin' all night, but I swear she was hidin' cards."

"Don't doubt it a bit," Longarm said with a chuckle as he headed for the cabin. "Wake me in a couple hours."

"Will do," Anderson said behind him as he climbed the stage, grunting with the effort.

Longarm took one more turn on guard duty before turning over the last watch to Anderson and tramping back into the cabin, in which a single lamp burned low on the single eating table. The cowboys and the gambler were sacked out on straw pallets on the floor. Danielle and Wilbur lay on their sides, tied wrists snugged against the ceiling joist. Wilbur's snores were almost inaudible amidst those of the other three men.

Curly Jim Hamer and his wife slept in the loft, and Curly Jim's snores were even louder than those of the drunken cowboys. Rye Spurlock slept in the only bed on the first floor, against the left wall and under a bleached bison skull, from the horns of which her skirt and blouse dangled.

Longarm looked around and decided that, since the girl was occupying only half the bed, he'd lie down beside her, which he did after quietly removing his hat and boots. He kept his gunbelt strapped to his waist, and the coach gun within fast, easy reach.

As he settled back against a pillow, Rye, who'd been sleeping beneath the thick buffalo robe, facing the wall, gave a sleepy groan and rolled toward him. She flung an arm across his chest and mashed her face against his ribs, giving another groan of contentment.

Her deep, regular breathing resumed.

Longarm draped an arm around the girl's shoulders, closed his eyes, and let sleep wash over him.

He woke to the loud clattering of a cast-iron stove lid, and jerked his head up, his heart thudding as he reached for the coach gun. Rye groaned and shifted her head against his ribs. Longarm froze when he saw Curly Jim's tongueless wife moving around in the kitchen behind him, stooping to light the stove.

Pale dawn light pushed through the cabin's dirty, sashed windows. The men on the floor sighed and groaned in protest at the woman's continued clamoring as she prepared breakfast. Longarm flung the buffalo robe aside, and dropped his feet to the floor.

Just outside the front door, boots thudded and a man sneezed. The latch was tripped, and the door squawked open. As Longarm pulled a boot on, he glanced up to see Anderson walk in on a chill blast of air.

"Everything quiet?" Longarm asked as the jehu stopped to kick at a tumbleweed clinging to his left leg.

"All quiet." Anderson gave the tumbleweed another kick, then stepped through the door. "Just me and the coyotes all night long, and I shore am hungry!"

Longarm stomped into his second boot, but he hadn't risen from the bed before the potbellied jehu gave a sharp grunt and stumbled forward. The man's chest opened, spurting blood, and a bullet slammed into a chimney pipe on the other end of the cabin with a flat *ping!*

Outside, a rifle cracked shrilly.

Two more bullets, followed by two more rifle cracks, tore through Anderson's chest. As the jehu screamed and stumbled into the cabin, dropping to his knees, Longarm grabbed his rifle. Levering a round into the chamber, he slammed the door shut with one shoulder as another bullet tore into the frame, spraying splinters.

He sidled up to the front wall on the other side of the door, then jerked the door open again suddenly, dropping to a knee in the opening and quickly firing four rounds into the yard.

As he fired, covering himself, he saw a couple of hazy figures in the dim light by the barn and one of the corrals. Smoke puffed from around the stage, and a bullet crashed through the window to Longarm's left. From the brick springhouse straight out from the cabin, someone yelped as though from a bullet burn, and then Longarm stepped back behind the door and slammed it closed.

Outside, rifles cracked—a half dozen or more—and bullets hammered the cabin's front wall and smashed through windows with the raucous screech of breaking glass. Bullets tore through the back windows as well, and the lead screamed around inside the cabin, sparking off the stove and hammering the adobe walls and the wooden furniture.

Rye Spurlock was on the floor beside the bed, clad in only her camisole and pantaloons, arms over her head. The two cowboys and the gambler—wearing only their longhandles, though Bill had donned his hat as well—had grabbed pistols and were hunkered down against the walls, wincing as bullets threaded the air around them.

Longarm couldn't see Hamer's wife from his position against the front wall between the door and a window. She was probably cowering in the small kitchen area between the stove and the eating table. Curly Jim himself suddenly barreled down the steep stairs from the loft, holding a Henry rifle in one hand and a Winchester '73 in the other. He wore baggy jeans and threadbare socks, his snakeskin suspenders drawn up over his worn red underwear top. His curly gray hair flopped in his eyes.

He was nearly down the stairs when a bullet tore through the window to his left. He winced and cursed loudly above the gunfire din as the slug tore a bloody red line across his upper left arm.

"Goddamn jackass sons o' two-bit whores!" he shouted as he hunkered down below and beside the cabin's east window. Leaning the Henry rifle against the wall, he levered a round into the Winchester's chamber.

Longarm waited for a slight gap in the shooting, then rose to a crouch, extended his own Winchester through the front window right of the door, and quickly levered three rounds into the yard, the rifle leaping and roaring in his hands. He doubted he hit anything, but he wanted to let the killers know they had a fight on their hands.

As he ejected a smoking round from the chamber, he crouched down beneath the window again and glanced at Johnny Anderson. The jehu lay belly down in the dirt just inside the door. Thick, dark blood was pooling around him. His shoulders didn't move. He wasn't breathing.

Longarm's heart hammered. Raw venom burned in his bowels. The Hutchins boys just weren't happy unless they were drilling someone in the back.

Longarm had just seated a fresh round and was about to return fire once more, when the shooting suddenly stopped. He froze, staring up at the broken window above his head, the torn flour-sack curtains blowing around on the chill morning wind.

"Come on outta there!" a distant voice called beneath the wind. "Come on outta there and bring the strongbox, and we'll see about lettin' ya live!"

Chapter 19

The invitation from the outlaw whom Longarm took to be Pink Hutchins settled like lead inside the bullet-riddled cabin. Longarm looked around.

Rye turned her head to peer up at him from beneath her arms. Her glassy eyes shone bright with fear. The cowboys and the gambler looked at him as well, their eyes fairly glowing with apprehension in the cabin's dim, smoke-webbed light.

A chunk of glass fell from a window frame and shattered on the earthen floor.

Curly Jim Hamer lifted his head to peer up over the sill of the window on the west side of the shack. "Like hell they will. They'll see about shootin' us so full o' holes, not a single one of us'd hold a thimbleful of water."

"Maybe not," the gambler, Hannibal Jenkins, said.

"Hamer's right," Longarm said, glancing down once more at Johnny Anderson's bloody back. The jehu's face was turned to one side, his eyes squeezed shut as though in excruciating agony. "We're gonna have to kill the sonso'bitches. Every last one."

He locked gazes with the other four men in the room. When he was sure he had their attention, he stood and thumbed fresh shells from his cartridge belt into his Winchester. "I'm gonna head on outside, try to work my way around 'em, kill as many as I can. In the meantime, you boys shoot through the windows. But mind your ammo. We want them to run out before we do."

He glanced at Rye, who was sitting with her back against the edge of the bed, and nudged her with his boot. "Crawl under the bed and stay there till I tell you to come out."

She seemed a little dazed as she looked around quickly, then, with an anxious little grunt, scuttled under the bed. Longarm grabbed the shotgun and, holding the big blaster in one hand, his Winchester in the other, stepped past the window, taking a another quick look outside as he did, noting the two gunmen hunkered down inside the big, main corral left of the barn, between the barn and the stagecoach. The horses milled in a frightened, ear-twitching group behind the outlaws, clumped against the corral's rear.

Minding the window left of the door, he strode quickly toward the door in the cabin's west wall—a shabby plank door that didn't appear to get much use, judging by the rusty, grime-caked hinges.

He glanced at Hamer on the other side of the room. "This door open?"

"Should. The old stable's out there."

Longarm reached for the latch. On the other side of the door, boots crunched gravel and men breathed raspily. The wan light filtering through the cracks between the door planks blinked.

Hunkered against the wall nearby, and dressed in silk longhandles and black socks with garters, the gambler said softly, anxiously, "Someone's out there."

Slowly, Longarm set his Winchester against the wall beside the door. Holding the shotgun in his right hand, he tripped the door latch with his left, and took one step back as he jerked the door wide.

Two men stood in the ruined, roofless stable before him. Both had shocked looks on their ruddy, unshaven faces, one wearing a green bandanna, the other a red one and clutching a rifle in his hands, the barrel angled up toward the soft morning sky.

"Oh, no," he said.

Longarm snugged the shotgun's stock against his hip, and the shotgun roared like a near thunderclap, causing the ground to jump and dust to sift down from the stable's ruined walls.

The outlaw with the red bandanna disappeared into the shadows of ruined stall partitions.

"No, wait!" screamed the outlaw with the green bandanna. At the same time, he lowered the barrel of his Spencer repeater.

"You wait, you walleyed son of a bitch."

With this last, Longarm tripped the coach gun's second barrel. The buckshot tore through the outlaw's middle. Bending forward, he was punched straight backward, howling, and bowled over an old rain barrel before hitting the straw-littered ground in a heap.

He rose up on an elbow, kicking and crying while holding his belly with his other hand. "Fucker . . . ya tore me in half!"

Outside the cabin, someone shouted. A rifle cracked. Then another. Longarm grabbed his Winchester and bolted into the stable, leaping the first, unmoving man he'd shot and yelling over his shoulder, "Hold the fort, boys!"

Then, as bullets buzzed around him, he hunkered down

behind the stable's low front adobe wall and breeched the coach gun. A couple of slugs hammered the bricks in front of him, spraying shards. Quickly, he thumbed out the spent eight-gauge wads, replaced them with fresh, and snapped the gun closed.

Setting the shotgun aside, he grabbed the Winchester, filled it with .44 shells from his cartridge belt, and seated a fresh shell in the breech. Outside, on the other side of the slowly brightening station yard, the owlhoots were yammering like coyotes as they peppered the station with rifle fire. The men inside the cabin were returning sporadic, halfhearted shots, but for the most part the Hutchins boys had them pinned down.

One lone shooter was firing from the backyard, probably hunkered down behind the wave-shaped rock ridge.

"Five left," Longarm muttered. "Damn doable."

He snaked the Winchester's barrel over the top of the crumbling adobe wall. An outlaw in a funnel-brimmed hat was hunkered beneath the stagecoach, extending a rifle toward the stable. Dust puffed from the rifle's maw, which the man was poking out between wheel spokes.

Longarm ducked as the slug slammed into the adobe wall with a hammering crash, blowing shards in all directions. Lifting his head and thrusting the rifle out over the wall once again, Longarm drew a bead on the head of the man beneath the stage. In the dim light, he could see only the tan of his hat and the pale oval of his face.

He fired two quick rounds.

Dust blew up around the man's head. He ducked. Longarm heard him curse beneath the rataplan of gunfire around the cabin. The lawman fired two more rounds, both of which blew up more dust or cracked a wheel spoke as the man crawled back and to one side.

Longarm cursed as he pulled the rifle back down behind the wall. He looked around. Grabbing both the rifle and the shotgun, he heaved himself to his feet and, crouching down below the ruined wall, tramped back to the stable's rear. There was only a hole where a door had been. He edged a look through it.

Nothing beyond it but rocks and sage, a few spindly cedars. The stage was straight across the yard from the stable's rear. Dust puffed beneath it as the gunman down there continued throwing lead toward the stable wall behind which Longarm had been hunkered.

The men in the corral were throwing all their lead at the front of the cabin, as was a man shooting from behind the springhouse just beyond the barn.

Hefting the Winchester in one hand and the coach gun in the other, Longarm sucked a breath and ran straight out from the end of the stable. He ducked behind an old stone stock tank, long unused, and crawled around to its far side.

Now, as he faced the yard, the stage was ahead of him and a little left. From this angle, he could see only the boots of the man shooting from beneath it. He waited until the man's fire died, indicating he was empty, then bolted out from behind the stock tank, making a beeline for the stage, which now stood between Longarm and the shooters inside the corral.

Halfway to the stage, Longarm took a knee, set the Winchester in the dirt, and brought the gut shredder to his shoulder, earing a hammer back. He bore down on the gent beneath the stage, who lay at an angle facing the stable, his right side facing Longarm.

The lawman didn't need to call out. The man, hastily thumbing fresh shells from his cartridge belt into the loading tube of his Henry repeater, glimpsed Longarm in the periphery of his vision. He jerked his head toward the lawman, and froze.

His teeth flashed, and he mouthed what was probably a curse, though Longarm couldn't hear it above the gunfire continuing all around. Longarm smiled shrewdly as the man shoved the loading tube home and jerked his rifle toward him.

Longarm's index finger drew back on the shotgun's trigger.

BOOM!

Longarm blinked as powder smoke wafted back over the broad double barrels to sting his eyes. When he opened them again, the gunman lay back against the wheel behind him, one shoulder propped against the spokes, his arms hanging slack, legs crossed at the ankles.

Blood matted his chest and belly, and dribbled from a half-dozen buckshot wounds in his ruddy, bony face. He stretched his lips back from his teeth and narrowed one eye painfully. His hands and feet jerked, and then his head rolled down and his right cheek dropped into the dirt.

A yell rose amidst the gunfire on the other side of the wagon. As two bullets tore through the stage's thin panels from the direction of the corral to screech through the air around him, Longarm left his rifle in the dirt and ran crouching toward the stage. He dove into the dust behind the stage's rear wheel.

More bullets tore through the wood above his head.

"Bastard's tryin' to get around us," a man's voice called. "Think he got Chance!"

"Chance is dead!" Longarm shouted, as a bullet barked off the iron-shod wheel six inches to his left. "And you last three sonso'bitches are about to join him, you don't throw down them guns."

"Why the fuck should we?"

"'Cause I'm a deputy U.S. marshal, and I'm only gonna give you this one chance. Then I'm burnin' you down like a barn in a Texas wildfire!"

"Here's what I think of your chance, you badge-totin' son of a bitch!"

Longarm glanced around the side of the wagon wheel. One of the two men in the corral ran toward the rear of the corral, where the horses were milling in tight circles, whinnying and swishing their tails, eyes wide as dinner plates. As the outlaw made his way toward them, the horses ran toward Longarm's side of the corral. The other man joined the first, both men waving rifles over their heads and whistling shrilly.

One barked like a dog, laughing.

The horses reared and buck-kicked, manes dancing.

Longarm aimed the shotgun over the top of the wagon wheel, then lowered it. The outlaws were too far away, shielding themselves with the circling, screaming remuda, for an accurate shot with the barn blaster.

As the two killers continued to hoot and holler, working the horses into a horrified lather and pushing them toward Longarm's side of the corral, the lawman glanced over his shoulder at his rifle lying in the dirt about twenty yards away. He'd just started to move toward the rifle when a bugling whinny rose from the corral, and he jerked a look over his shoulder.

A big, black, white-socked horse leaped off its rear hooves and hammered its broad chest into the corral fence. The top two rails cracked beneath the big animal's bulk and fell in pieces as the black leaped into the yard.

"Ah, shit," Longarm groaned.

He dropped down behind the wheel as the horse stormed

toward him, swerving at the last second to avoid the stage. The ground beneath Longarm's boots jerked and pitched as the other horses leaped what was left of the corral fence and stormed toward him, snorting and screaming, the thuds of their pounding hooves sounding like thunder.

Longarm dropped the coach gun and slid his .44 from its holster.

Smoke puffed over the bounding horses, the bullets whistling around Longarm's head. Several of them hammered the stage. As the two dozen tightly grouped horses thundered toward him, he saw that the two killers were running along behind and sort of to one side, using the horses for cover while flinging lead toward the stage.

Longarm fired two rounds in the air, and as the remuda swerved as one out away from him, a bullet barked into the iron-shod wheel in front of his face while another drilled the stage with a thud that was lost in the thunder of the fleeing horses. One of the outlaws—a man with long red hair and a beard, and wearing a knee-length deerskin jacket—fired another shot over the rump of the last horse in the herd.

As the slug curled the air beside him, Longarm threw himself beneath the stage. He crawled quickly under the rear luggage boot and extended the .44 straight out in front of him.

The last horses were just clearing the back of the stage. A pinto went buck-kicking off to Longarm's left, and in the dust of its passing, the long-haired gent knelt aiming his Winchester toward the stage. Another man—short, potbellied, and wearing a gray sombrero and a billowing pink neckerchief—crouched off to the man's right, two pistols leaping and roaring in his hands.

As the slugs plunked into the dust in front of Longarm,

the lawman fired two quick rounds. The long-haired gent flew straight back in the dust, screaming and flinging another shot skyward. He hadn't hit the ground before Longarm whipped the .44 to his left, drew a bead on the other man, and fired two more rounds.

The potbellied gent yelped and, triggering one shot into the ground and another into the air, jerked backward as though he'd just been hit hard in the face. His gray sombrero fell down his back, revealing his thin hair, which was red, but a shade darker than that of the other hombre.

Somehow, he remained on his knees.

His black eyes found Longarm, his pink neckerchief blowing in the wind. He dropped his chin, glanced at the two bloody holes in his sheepskin vest, beneath the bandoliers crisscrossed on his chest, and looked again at Longarm.

"You kilt me, you son of a bitch."

His arms dropped, and he dropped both guns in the dirt. But he continued to kneel there, shoulders wobbling precariously, lower jaw hanging.

Longarm crawled out from beneath the stage. He holstered his empty .44 and picked up the coach gun. Holding the shotgun low across his thighs, he said, "Pink Hutchins?"

For a second, he thought the outlaw was dead. But then the man nodded weakly, and rolled his black, oily eyes toward the other man, who lay unmoving on the ground to his right. "That's my brother. V . . . Vernon."

Pink Hutchins's voice cracked, and his eyes scrunched with emotion. "You kilt us both, you bastard!"

Pink mewled with rage, his face and mouth twisted bizarrely.

The outlaw leader's thin, dusty hair blew in the wind, and blood continued to pump from the holes in his chest, just below his billowing neckerchief. He had a pistol wedged in his pants over his belly, and slowly, deliberately, he reached for it.

"Nah. Don't do that," Longarm warned. "You're a dead man, Pink. I'd hate to have to desecrate your corpse."

Pink Hutchins screamed with horror and fury as he began to pull the pistol from his pants. "Ah, shit," Longarm said as he lifted the shotgun's barrel and blew the man's head off.

He turned away quickly from the bleeding corpse, and started walking slowly, weakly back toward the station, the shake roof of which the morning light now dusted with gold. A tall man was walking toward him, holding a rifle over each shoulder.

Longarm stopped as Curly Jim Hamer walked up, canting his head to one side, his expression faintly incredulous, questioning.

Longarm shouldered the coach gun. "That's about it for out here."

He glanced toward the springhouse. The man who'd been shooting from behind the small, brick building now lay on his back in the dust behind it, limbs spread as though he'd been dropped from the sky.

"There oughta be one more," Longarm said to Hamer.

"There oughta be, but there ain't." Hamer smiled, his eyes flashing shrewdly under the gray curls hanging in his eyes. "My squaw took him as he tried comin' in the back door. Awful mess a forty-five makes at close range"—he winced as he glanced at what remained of Pink Hutchins—"though not near as awful as that eight-gauge makes."

Then the station manager scowled and shook his head as he glanced back at the cabin. "But they sure cleaned ole Johnny's clock. I best get back and tend him."

As Hamer turned and walked back toward the cabin, Rye Spurlock came out, shoving her mussed hair back from her eyes. She was still clad in her pantaloons and camisole as she strolled out to where Longarm stood in the middle of the yard, shouldering the big shotgun.

"You okay, Longarm?"

He sighed, feeling the fatigue of the long journey and the end of another assignment down deep in his bones. There was also the heavy, cloying sadness of losing a good man and a new friend in Johnny Anderson.

"I reckon I been better."

Rye wrapped her arms around Longarm's waist and laid her head against his chest. The two just stood there as the morning wind shepherded tumbleweeds around them and gradually dispersed the rotten-egg odor of powder smoke.

Epilogue

"Well, I sure am sorry you couldn't find ole Bob," Longarm said, nuzzling Rye Spurlock's plump left breast.

The sexy blonde rose slowly, quiveringly up and down on his anvil-hard cock in their shared room at the Utah House Hotel in Crow Canyon in western Colorado.

Straddling the lawman, Rye rose up on her knees and reached under her bottom to tickle Longarm's shaft with her fingers.

She said in a thin, passionate whisper, "Oh, I reckon it just wasn't meant to be. Bob musta gone down to Arizona for the winter or some such. He was a real sissy when it came to cold and snowy weather. Besides, if I'd found him, we wouldn't have these last few days together, Longarm . . . and we wouldn't be traveling together back to Denver."

"Touché," Longarm said as the girl settled her silky, wet snatch down on his crotch once more, sort of squirming around to increase their rapturous pleasure.

She sighed throatily, squeezing her eyes closed and hardening her jaws. Her hair danced across Longarm's broad, naked chest.

Earlier, Longarm had fetched the trussed-up sharp-shooter, Charley Dodd, and hauled him with the other two prisoners to Crow Canyon in the stage, which the lawman had had to jehu solo after the death of Johnny Anderson at the hands of the Pink Hutchins Bunch.

Longarm, his three prisoners, Rye Spurlock, the two cowboys, the gambler, and the gold bullion had all pulled into Crow Canyon the very next day after the gun battle. That was nearly a week ago now, and with Charley Dodd and Danielle and Wilbur awaiting the circuit judge in the Crow Canyon hoosegow, Longarm was just taking a little breather before heading back to Denver and, likely, another assignment from the desk of Billy Vail.

He didn't get many days off, so he decided to take his time heading back to work.

Rye had decided to try her luck in the big city snugged at the foot of the Front Range, and Longarm saw no reason they shouldn't ride together. If the last few days in the Utah House Hotel here in Crow Canyon were any indication, it would be a delightful trek.

"Oh, Lordy, Gus," Rye said, grinding up and down and shivering as though chilled, her gold-blond curls dancing about her lightly tanned cheeks. "Oh . . . oh, *Gawwwd.* . . . !"

Longarm took the girl's right nipple between his lips as they came together in one long, delightful spasm that shook the entire bed and caused a man in the next room to pound on the wall and yell, "For Chrissakes, would you two give it a *rest* in there? I turned in late and I'd like to sleep *in* this mornin'!"

Longarm reached up and placed his hand over Rye's mouth as, oblivious of their neighbor's complaint, she continued to sob and mewl as she sank, spent, toward Long-arm's chest. When he himself had finished his pleasure, he rolled the still-quivering girl onto her back, smoothed her hair back from her warm cheeks, and kissed her gently on her bee-stung lips.

"Ready fer breakfast, Miss Rye?"

"No!" Rye balked, keeping her eyes closed but hooking one leg over Longarm's. "Let's stay here all day and fuck like minks!"

Longarm chuckled. "Temptin'. Mighty temptin', Miss Rye. But I done rented us horses for the trip to Denver. We'll have plenty of time to frolic out in the tall and uncut, where we won't be disturbing any whiskey drummers."

"I sell schoolbooks!" the man in the next room objected.

"Or schoolbook drummers," Longarm corrected.

"You go on ahead." Rye lifted her head to kiss Longarm's chest, then turned onto her side, drawing her knees up toward her breasts. "You done kilt me, and I'm gonna need thirty winks to get my strength back."

Longarm kissed the side of her left breast. Damn, it was hard to leave the bed of such a creature!

Reluctantly, he dropped his legs to the floor and poured water for a whore's bath. When he'd finished bathing and dressing, Rye had begun to stir once more, and suddenly one long, naked leg dropped out of the quilts and blankets, and a fine-boned foot hit the floor.

"Oh, I reckon all that fuckin' does work up an appetite, Longarm," the girl said, sitting up and rubbing the sleep from her eyes.

"I'll see ya downstairs," Longarm told her as he donned his hat and pulled the door closed behind him. "Don't tarry. I'm starvin'!"

In the saloon downstairs, Longarm ordered a cup of coffee and a shot of rye to wait for the girl who, appropriately, shared the name of his favorite beverage. He sat at a table near the popping woodstove, enjoying the heat, for early winter had come to the central Rockies. Outside, a thin dusting of snow shone bright on the sunlit main street as well as on the rugged nearby mountains, and a chill breeze howled under the hotel's eaves.

The saloon was surprisingly busy for eight o'clock in the morning, though one set of gamblers, near the broad stairs running up the back of the room, had obviously been there all night. They were red-eyed, and their clothes were rumpled. A couple of the five players were flipping coins and laying down cards as though their hands were made of lead.

The rest of the customers appeared to be rock breakers from the local mine. They all wore beards, fur hats, heavy, soiled clothes, and stout-soled hobnailed boots. They owned the boisterous air of men who'd worked all night, and they were throwing back drinks and conversing loudly in what sounded like Russian. Two of them had tired-looking working girls on their laps, and two more, sitting near Longarm and the stove, were smoking pipes, playing cribbage, and conversing in the lilting cadences of one of the Nordic tongues.

Longarm poured his rye into his coffee and stirred the heady-smelling concoction with his cigar. He took a sip of the brew, then another, smacked his lips with approval, and lit the cigar, taking a long, deep puff into his lungs.

He'd just tossed the match onto the floor when the bell jangled over the front door. Longarm was facing the room's rear, his back to the stove, so he glanced with vague curiosity into the backbar mirror to see who'd entered the saloon from behind him.

He looked once, saw a tall, black-hatted figure in a fur coat. He looked away. A half wink later, his gaze darted back to the mirror and held there, eyes widening, his lower jaw dropping in shock.

The tall figure grew slowly larger in the mirror as the man's footsteps—or foot*step* rather, coupled with the raspy drag of his second, gimpy foot—moved toward the front of the saloon. When the man was directly to Longarm's right, the lawman swiveled his head around to inspect the newcomer more closely.

As he took in the black clothes under the shaggy, charcoal, thigh-length wolf coat, his eyes roamed around the tall, lean, dark-skinned, hawk-nosed figure until he saw that the man was holding his left arm straight down at his side as he dragged the heel of his right boot. He wore a black glove on his right hand. He held the hand down low against his thigh, all the fingers and the thumb fully extended.

None of the fingers moved, and the entire hand itself seemed to be made of . . . well, it seemed to be made of wood.

Longarm's temples throbbed. His throat grew dry, his tongue thick.

For a moment, he wondered if all the injuries he'd incurred over the past week, starting with his tumble down the stone ledge preceding the snakebite and his introduction to Rye Spurlock, hadn't softened his head, caused him to conjure fanciful, dreamlike images. But then the barman, who'd been sweeping lazily behind the bar, sauntered over to the tall, black-clad, limping hombre and asked him what he wanted.

The man said something in a peculiar, grunting voice. He sounded as though he were speaking around a mouthful of broken teeth.

"Christ, amigo," the bartender said. "If you're gonna talk so damn strange, at least speak up so's I can hear you!"

"Da gurl!" the man yelled, slapping his stiff hand on the bar for emphasis.

A shrill scream echoed around the saloon, and Longarm's gaze jerked to the stairs on the left side of the bar. Rye Spurlock stood two thirds of the way down the staircase, one hand on the rail and crouching forward at the waist as she stared wide-eyed at the specter at the bar.

"Oh, no!" she cried.

Longarm bolted to his feet, overturning his steaming coffee cup. He grabbed his .44, but not before the improbable nightmare figure before him had moved with surprising speed, grunting and dragging his gimpy leg, to the bottom of the stairs.

Rye wheeled, and in her haste she tripped over her own feet and dropped to her hip. Pulling himself up the stairs with one hand on the rail, the stranger was on Rye in seconds.

"Hold it!" Longarm called, crouching and raising the Colt.

He held fire as the tall, hawk-faced man hauled Rye to her feet, shielding his body with hers, though the girl's head came up only to the tall man's neck. Snarling and spitting like some wild beast, he wrapped his right arm around Rye's neck.

In his gloved hand was a pearl-handled bowie knife. The pearl handle glistened in stark contrast to the man's black glove. He drew the knife back close to the girl's throat. He opened his oddly shaped mouth and smiled, showing a handful of crooked, tobacco-stained teeth.

"Anyone tries to stop me," he spat out as though both jaws were broken, "I cut her head off and you keep for trophy!" He wheezed a weird laugh as his black crow eyes swept the room, but lingered for the most part on Longarm, the only one in the place with his gun drawn.

"Put down!" the stranger grunted loudly as Rye sobbed in his grasp. He stared hard at Longarm. "I take her, or *no one* take her!"

Longarm's heart skipped a beat. Rye stared at him from the stairs. Her eyes were sad and desperate, and her mouth was stretched wide as she cried almost too shrilly to be heard.

Longarm stared at the knife. It was about a half inch from the girl's throat. Even if he was able to drill a .44 slug through the stranger's head, the man could still cut her fatally.

Longarm held up his left hand, palm out, then depressed the Colt's hammer and set the gun on the table. Holding his arms up, he stepped back away from it.

"Easy, friend," he told the obviously insane stranger. "Be careful with that knife."

The man laughed again. Pushing Rye down the stairs in front of him, he stayed close to her, keeping the knife so close to Rye's neck that Longarm was sure she could feel the edge raking her skin.

The other men in the bar had frozen in their chairs as they watched the tall stranger and the girl descend the stairs and start toward the front. A couple of the Russians muttered exclamations in their natives tongues, but most of the men in the room were so silent that Longarm thought he could hear their cigars and pipes burning.

The apron stood frozen behind the bar, fists on his hips, scowling incredulously.

Longarm shuttled his gaze between Rye's horrified eyes and the killer's black, glistening ones. He waited for an opportunity to grab his .44 from the table and start blasting, but he never got it.

And then the tall man and the girl were at the front door.

"Anyone comes to the door before I'm outta town with dis one here," he said in his strange accent that seemed due more to some physical peculiarity than to the fact that he obviously owned a good bit of Apache blood, "and I cut her *head* off!"

Rye and Longarm shared one last agonized glance, and then the tall man jerked the door open, pulled her through it, closed it behind him, and disappeared.

Longarm grabbed the .44 as the saloon crowd lifted a collective roar of exasperation. The lawman tripped over a chair and dropped to a knee. Cursing, he pushed himself back to his feet and ran to the door.

He'd no sooner pulled it open, the bell jangling raucously, than the stranger seemed to materialize out of thin air, facing Longarm from the other side of the threshold. He had a strange, sallow, wooden look on his face.

Longarm frowned as he held his cocked Colt out in front of his belly, aiming at the stranger's chest. The man stumbled forward, and his face twisted, eyes spoking. Holding the Colt firmly in front of him, Longarm stepped back and to one side, and the tall, black-clad specter stumbled into the room a few feet past the lawman.

The man's own pearl-gripped bowie knife was lodged hilt deep in his back.

The stranger twisted around, grunting and snarling and futilely reaching for the firmly embedded blade. Then his arms dropped to his sides. His chin dropped to his chest.

He fell straight down to the floor, smashing his nose against the scarred planks. A loud thump and a moist crunching sound echoed around the saloon.

Longarm glanced to his right. Rye stood in the open doorway, looking stricken. She stared in horror at the long, black-clad body in front of her.

Longarm crouched and, planting a boot on the stranger's left shoulder for leverage, jerked the bowie knife from his back. Then he hooked his boot under the man's shoulder and rolled him over.

The black, death-glazed eyes stared up at Longarm. The stranger's nose was bent to one side. Blood trickled from his nostrils. His scraggly teeth shone in a death snarl.

His stiff right hand lay out to one side, open palm facing the ceiling.

Longarm glanced at Rye. She turned to him. Suddenly, the fear in her eyes was gone. Anger lifted a flush in her smooth cheeks.

She pursed her lips and wrinkled her pretty, blond brows, her full breasts rising sharply beneath her red calico blouse.

She didn't say anything, so Longarm felt obliged to. "Weed Cormorant, I assume?"

Rye blew her hair out of her eyes. "Sure ain't Santy Claus!"

Watch for

LONGARM AND SIERRA SUE

the 371st novel in the exciting LONGARM
series from Jove

Coming in October!

And don't miss

**LONGARM AND
THE LONE STAR TRACKDOWN**

Longarm Giant Edition 2009

Available from Jove in October!

LONGARM

GIANT-SIZED ADVENTURE FROM
AVENGING ANGEL LONGARM.

BY TABOR EVANS

penguin.com/actionwesterns

M456AS0409

Jove Westerns put the "wild"
back into the Wild West.

LONGARM
by Tabor Evans

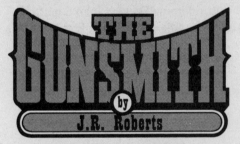

THE GUNSMITH
by
J.R. Roberts

SLOCUM by
JAKE LOGAN

Don't miss these exciting, all-action series!
penguin.com/actionwesterns

M11G0808

Sandy Public Library

Penguin Group (USA) Online

What will you be reading tomorrow?

Tom Clancy, Patricia Cornwell, W.E.B. Griffin,
Nora Roberts, William Gibson, Robin Cook,
Brian Jacques, Catherine Coulter, Stephen King,
Dean Koontz, Ken Follett, Clive Cussler,
Eric Jerome Dickey, John Sandford,
Terry McMillan, Sue Monk Kidd, Amy Tan,
John Berendt…

You'll find them all at
penguin.com

Read excerpts and newsletters,
find tour schedules and reading group guides,
and enter contests.

Subscribe to Penguin Group (USA) newsletters
and get an exclusive inside look
at exciting new titles and the authors you love
long before everyone else does.

PENGUIN GROUP (USA)
us.penguingroup.com

M224G1107